The Unexpected Match

L. Clara

Contents

Trigger Warning

Include but are not limited to:

Divorce

Manipulation

Cheating (not main love interests)

Abuse

Death

Murder

Domestic Violence

Anxiety

Depression

Attempted Suicide

Sexually explicit scenes

Please feel free to reach out to L. Clara at lcturnspages@gmail.com with any questions regarding triggers.

Note from the author

If you or anyone you know is a victim of domestic violence, please reach out for help.

National Domestic Violence Hotline 1-800-799-7233 Text "START" to 88788

If you or anyone you know is struggling with suicidal thoughts or going through a crisis, you can call or text the 988 Lifeline, which provides 24/7, free, and confidential support. Call or text them by dialing 988 or live message/chat with them at their website: https://988lifeline.org

This book does not depict a healthy open/polyamorous relationship and should not be taken as a guide on how to open a relationship.

Playlist

Our Song – Taylor Swift

I Got The Boy – Jana Kramer

Low (feat. T-Pain) Flo Rida

Terrified – Katharine McPhee & Jason Reeves

Trustfall – P!nk

Last Kiss – Taylor Swift

Suffocate – Kayzo, Bad Omens

I Hate Everything About You – Three Days Grace

Kiss With A Fist – Florence + The Machine

You should be sad – Halsey

I Won't See You Tonight Part 1 – Avenged Sevenfold

Independence Day – Martina McBride

I'll Be There for You – The Rembrandts

HOLD YOU DOWN – X Ambassadors

Whiskey – Jana Kramer

Animal I Have Become – Three Days Grace

Photograph – Ed Sheeran

The Reason – Hoobastank

Still Falling For You – Ellie Goulding

Miracle – Shinedown

Dedication

To my grandmother: MomMom, if you really thought my first book had too much of "the sex" close this one and don't look back.

Glossary

Howya: Hi, Hello

Tá brón orm: My apologies/I'm sorry

A mhuirnín: Darling

A thaisce: Treasure

Mo stór: My Treasure

Boyo: boy or man

Bodach: Low-life

Fine-thing: Good looking woman/man

Tá tú foirfe: You are perfect

Mo ghrá: My Love

Táim i ngrá leat: I'm in love with you

Mo shíorghrá: Eternal Love

F ive years ago

After five years, today is the day! We're getting married!

Attending high school together and being separated by several cities at different colleges, it feels surreal, as if this is the path we have always been on since the day we met. Before we left for college, Andy confessed that he knew he would marry me one day, but part of me didn't believe him. I knew the statistics of long-distance relationships, especially in those first few years of college.

Eventually, we couldn't take it anymore, and Andy transferred to Lyndon University just outside Central Falls to be with me. I was ecstatic, and from that moment on, I had no doubt that we would last. The odds were against us, yet here we stand.

I stare into the dark eyes of my high school sweetheart, Andy James. His soft blond hair is mussed like he ran his fingers through it too many times while waiting for our moment. This man is so beautiful; he is mine, and I am his.

"Do you, Andy Michael James, take Hadley Veronica Lancaster to be your lawfully wedded wife?" Pastor Giovanni asks while Andy and I gaze into each other's eyes at the front of the church before our family and friends.

After hearing Andy say, "I do," the rest of the ceremony is a blur. I know I recite my vows, but after that, everything is a joyous haze.

We are herded around with the wedding party for pictures. Thankfully, it is a cooler day for June. If it was any warmer, my makeup would melt off. A nice breeze blows just enough to keep everyone comfortable while we are instructed on who is next. Between the bridesmaids and groomsmen, we have six people besides Andy and me to get photographs of. Then our parents and grandparents are on top of that.

I'm ready for a drink once we finally make our grand entrance. I love Andy and my family—honestly, I do—but damn. A girl can only take so much.

Thankfully, Ryan, my best friend since junior high, has a screwdriver ready for me when Andy and I make it to our table. She looks beautiful in the dress we chose for her as my maid of honor. Her shoulder-length blonde hair is curled in soft waves, and her peach-colored smokey eye that she chose makes her milk chocolate eyes pop.

"Congrats, babe!" She smiles as she hands me my drink.

"I am so happy!" I shout gleefully, even if I am a little buzzed.

Andy and I sway back and forth to "Our Song" by Taylor Swift, lost in each other.

With the biggest grin plastered on his face, he brushes his lips against my ear. "I love you so much, Hadley."

We sing along with the music until it fades into the next song, and most of our guests join us on the dance floor.

My man's Tardis-blue tux is taut over his broad chest and muscular arms. He looks sexy as hell. He spins me in a circle around the dance floor, his arms wrapped tight around my waist, keeping me close. The evening fades into night, and night fades into the early morning hours before the reception guests part ways.

We just signed on our first house two days ago, right in the heart of Central Falls. Boxes have yet to be unpacked. We had no time between being handed the keys and walking down the aisle. I'm nervous to get home tonight. We've made love before, but this feels different. Like it's the first time for the rest of our lives.

Jana Kramer had it wrong. I had the boy, but I also get the man.

Connor

It's been a week since I got the call. I haven't come to terms with the news. Colin was so young, only twenty-nine. This shite just isn't fair. He had so much more to do in this life.

I step off the plane to see my baby sister and nephew. Alannah's cherry-colored hair is tied in a low knot at the base of her neck. Her jade-green eyes are hidden behind a pair of sunglasses that are too large for her face. The evidence of tears is clear in Sean's eyes, which look bloodshot; I can see the puffiness in both of their faces, even behind her sunglasses.

My brother-in-law is dead, killed instantly in a head-on collision with a drunk driver. The driver suffered the same fate, though I don't know how to feel about that. It seems as though she got off easy, yet her family doesn't deserve the same pain we're going through.

No matter how much we begged and pleaded for Alannah to return to Ireland, she refused. She couldn't uproot her boyo. I can't blame her. He's been through more than anyone at eight years old should ever have to endure.

I made a promise to Alannah when we were kids. I will always see her as a baby, even now at twenty-eight. Being the oldest, with a twelve-year age gap, I had to care for her growing up, especially after Ma passed away when Alannah was two. Da had to work two jobs just to keep us afloat, so Alannah was mine from then on.

The promise from our childhood seemed like it shouldn't even need to be uttered. Knowing how stubborn my baby sister is, though, she wouldn't have asked if I hadn't vocalized it. She knew I would drop everything and be there if she ever needed me. There was no question when she told me the news; I needed to be here. It took a week to finalize the details of replacing my CEO position at O'Sullivan TeicNet. Now that I'm here, I can concentrate on helping my family recover from the grief of losing Colin.

I didn't expect to stay as long as I have, but the longer I am around Sean, the harder it is to say goodbye. Eventually, finding a position with DL Technologies Inc. has allowed me to stay put and continue helping my sister raise Sean.

I had to rush home from the gym. Andy and I have made it a point to have a date night each Friday night at eight p.m., and I'm cutting it so close to being able to get ready by the time he gets home.

My session with Kat went over what we planned, though if I'm honest, it usually does. We always get to talking and forgot that we're supposed to be working out together. We have gotten so close since meeting at the gym after I decided to quit my job.

Andy and I wanted a child so badly that we decided that I should take on less stress, which led to me leaving my dream career as a teacher, at least for now. I will say it's been less stressful with no asshole boss micromanaging my every breath, but I'm not the biggest fan of having to rely solely on Andy for everything.

"Hadley?" I hear him shouting from the foyer as I put the last touches on my makeup.

Taking one last glance in the mirror, I admire my form-fitting teal dress. It hugs my soft curves in all the right ways. My dark hair is in romantic curls and my makeup is applied perfectly, just enough to brighten my complexion with a golden smokey eye, which makes my baby blues pop. I smirk at myself before heading out to see my man.

"Coming, honey!" I shout and giggle to myself.

That's what she said.

I walk down the stairs to find him leaning against the doorframe.

"Hi, handsome! How was your day?"

I admire him as I approach. His broad chest fills out his navy suit so deliciously.

"It was fine. Let's go. We're going to be late."

Andy opens the door and motions for me to walk out to the car.

"I told you I had reservations at Providence," he scolds as he closes his door, leaving me to rush to the passenger side.

"I know, honey. I'm sorry. I really didn't mean to be late." I close the passenger door and buckle myself in as he stares at me. "We should still make it on time, though. The restaurant called to confirm our reservation today, and it's for eight-fifteen. They said that there was an issue with their booking system and they couldn't get us our usual time."

I'm shocked when he turns his cheek just as I lean in to kiss him, and my stomach flips unpleasantly. It's our tenth and fifth anniversary tonight: ten from when we first started dating, and five since we got married. Anxiety rushes into my chest as I feel a dread that makes my stomach drop. I know something is wrong; I just can't put my finger on what.

He is way too quiet on the drive over to the restaurant. There is a tension in his jaw that just doesn't make sense. His hands are gripping the steering wheel so tightly, his knuckles turn white. Usually, we chat about his day and how work has been. He has become so much more distant lately, ignoring calls or texts and canceling plans at the last minute. I thought work was just becoming overwhelming, but now I'm not sure what it could be.

We arrive at Providence, and the valet greets us upon exiting the car.

"Hi, Jim!" I smile at the thin older gentleman who has been here since our first date after we got married.

"Hi, sweet girl. How's my favorite couple? It's your anniversary tonight, isn't it?"

Jim is always a staple in our Friday night dates, constantly checking in on us. He is simply the sweetest. His thinning hair has gone white in the years since we started dining there.

Andy walks off quietly, and I notice he is looking at his phone with a smile on his face that I haven't seen in a while. Maybe I'm just overreacting.

"Aww, Jim! You remembered?" I wrap my arms around him in a quick hug. "We're good. How are you? Did your daughter have your grandbaby yet?"

After a few moments of conversation catching up on the past week with Jim, we head inside at ten after eight. As usual, the maître d' greets us with a friendly smile and walks us right to our table.

Once the wine has been served, I attempt to coax Andy into a conversation.

"How was your day? Did you get the contract you've been working on signed today?" I ask, offering a sweet smile.

"Yeah." He glances at me with no emotion, meeting my gaze before he continues with the confidence of Shenzi just before Mufasa showed up to rescue Simba and Nala.

Then he says the five words every woman dreads.

"Listen, we need to talk."

My heart starts pounding in my chest. This can't be happening.

I can barely get an "okay" out, and just nod for him to continue.

"I love you, Had. I will love you forever, but I'm not really happy. I haven't been for a while," he sighs.

It takes several moments for the words to sink in.

Our entire relationship flashes before my eyes with thoughts of where I went wrong. All I have ever tried to do is take care of him. My heart lurches in my chest, the shock internally tearing me apart.

"You're leaving me?" I choke on a sob that has been trying to claw its way out of my throat.

My eyes drop to the floor, confusion over what has transpired in the last twenty-four hours consuming me. I lose all sense of my surroundings as panic clouds my vision. I can't breathe.

"What? No." He shakes his head and is beside me with his arms around me instantly. "I don't want to leave you. I just want to experience...more."

"I don't understand," I tremble out, the words barely audible through my shallow breaths. "What *more* could you want to experience?"

He stares at me for several moments. Glancing around the room, he looks like he's having trouble finding the words.

That is, until he blurts out, "I need more in bed. There is just so much more to explore than what you can provide me. I mean, you say you'll try anything at least once, but the last time I tried to fuck your ass, you pushed me away."

Taking a quick breath, he continues.

"I told you, I love you. But you can't tell me you're satisfied."

My eyes widen, and I laugh, the tears drying.

"This is a joke, right?" I shake my head as if to clear the conversation from recent memory. "We just had sex last night. I have had every first with you, and I've never been against anything you've wanted to try."

Andy blanches.

"Lower your voice." He glances around, as if we're close enough for anyone else to hear our conversation. "We've only ever been with one another. Don't you want to explore more? I told you, I don't want to leave you."

I can't find the words to respond. He takes that as an invitation to continue.

"I just want to have a well-rounded life experience. I think we need to open our marriage. We will both be able to get that experience while still having each other."

My world as I know it comes crumbling down around me.

"I love you, Hadley, but I need this freedom for us to work." His voice is quiet, but firm.

The only way to keep my husband is to allow him to sleep with other people?

What. The. Fuck?

What. The. Fuck?

Chapter Two

F our months later

I'm lying in a fetal position on my couch yet again.

This has been my default position since Andy told me he needed our marriage to be open. That I wasn't satisfying him enough in the bedroom. I have only left the couch to go to the bathroom and get the occasional snack since we got home that night.

I must have dozed off because I wake up to Kat and Ryan standing over me. Kat nestles her way onto the couch and pulls me into an embrace.

"The last four months have been worse than when my grandpa passed away, you guys." Once again, I'm crying to Ryan and Kat.

"Oh, babe, we will get you through this. Is he still seeing her?" Kat asks me with her arm around my shoulders.

Ryan is on my other side, sandwiching me between my best friends and handing us each a whiskey shot.

"Yeah. He's been at Naomi's house most nights since I agreed to open the marriage." I down the shot in one gulp before slumping against Kat's chest, her teal hair hanging loose and tickling my neck. "I don't think I can do this anymore."

I have lost so much weight over the last months that the liquor is going straight to my head.

"You have lovely pillows. Have I ever told you that?"

Ryan snorts. "As much as I agree that Pickle's tits are delightful, no, we are not doing this. He wants to open the marriage, so you are going to go out there and get so much dick that he won't be able to satisfy you anymore."

Kat jerks away from me, throwing a pillow at Ryan's head. "Will you stop calling me 'Pickle'? It's the worst nickname ever!"

She pulls me back against her chest as Ryan continues to rant.

"You know what? Fuck this. Where is your phone?" She lets out an annoyed huff.

She grabs my phone from the coffee table and taps on the screen for several moments. Her chocolate eyes hold a mischievous sparkle before she turns my phone around. On the screen is a Tinder profile with my name and picture.

"Oh, shit," Kat gasps. "You really think she's ready for this?"

"What? No! I can't do this!" I groan, realizing I'm still snuggled up against Kat's breasts.

I sit up quickly when I see Ryan is swiping right and occasionally left.

"What are you doing, Ry?!" I shout at her.

"Oh, he's cute. Don't you think, Pickle?" Ryan turns my phone to Kat, avoiding my reach to sass her way through my sex life. "Oh, no. *Here* he is. This is the one! Look at that silver fox! And he's a transplant from Ireland! Bitch, you are going to swoon over that accent!"

I jump up and swipe my phone from her to make it stop. She laughs at me before giving me a hug.

"I love you both, but I can't do this." I motion to my phone just as it dings with a notification.

You have a new match!

I look between the two of them before unlocking my phone. I swiped right on the silver fox when I snatched my phone from Ryan, and he matched with me. Already?

Another notification comes through, which I promptly ignore as I say goodnight to my friends and usher them out the door before they can come up with any other "helpful" ideas.

I'm sitting on the couch with a glass of wine about an hour later when another notification comes through.

Two new messages.

I have to admit, from the brief glance I got of his photo when I nearly tackled Ryan to get my phone back, the man is sexy. It isn't just that he has the silver fox thing going for him. His eyes are a delicious amber color that reminds me of leaves changing in the fall.

Okay, fine. I stared at his photo for about thirty minutes after my girls left.

I could get lost in those eyes. At forty-one, he's fourteen years my senior. Should I really be as intrigued by this beautiful specimen of a man as I am? Curiosity gets the better of me, and instead of just deleting the app, I want to see what that beautiful man has to say. With trembling hands, I tap on the notification to open the messages.

Connor:

Howya, a mhuirnín!

Connor:

I must admit, when my nephew suggested I download this app, I did not expect to come across someone as breathtakingly beautiful as you.

My heart skips a beat. I expected something forward and someone just looking for a hookup. I didn't expect such a sweet message.

I take a deep breath to steady myself in my resolve before tapping out a message on the screen.

Chapter Three

Connor

I was annoyed when Sean suggested I download this app. I did it just to shut him up. But fuck, this woman.

Her profile says her husband wanted to open up their relationship. What kind of thick bodach would want anyone but her? She is everything.

Well, thank you. I didn't necessarily expect a message as sweet as that to be the first one I opened. I'm sorry, though. I'm unfamiliar with the first thing you said?

I chuckle as I type out a response.

I guess you can take the man out of Ireland, but you can't take Ireland out of the man. Howya means "hi" or "how are you" & a mhuirnín is a term of endearment we use back home. It means "darling."

Her response comes more quickly this time.

Hadley:

Oh! That is beautiful! I'm OK. Just having a glass of wine and reading a book. How are you tonight?

I frown at my phone.

Connor:

Just OK? How can we make that better, a mhuirnín? I'm having a much better night now. What are you reading?

Hadley:

Honestly, I'm not quite sure how to make it better. Although you asking how to made me smile. I'm reading my favorite book, Finding Each Other by Sara Hurst. I've read it so many times I can probably recite it without reading the actual pages, but I can't get enough of the characters and the story.

Connor:

I'm glad I can make you smile, a mhuirnín. I'll look into that book if it's your favorite. (wink emoji)

Hadley:

I'd offer to lend you my copy, but as silly as it is, it's a "comfort blanket" of sorts. LOL.

Connor:

You're lómhara, a mhuirnin.

Hadley:

I had to Google that one. I'm hoping the transla-
tion is right. Precious? You're kind. I have a thing
for romance books. I love getting lost in those
worlds.

Connor:

Besides Finding Each Other, what is another
book I should check out? I'd like to learn more
about what you enjoy!

I smile to myself as I add *Finding Each Other* to my Amazon cart.

We continue chatting late into the night, but eventually, the need for sleep becomes overwhelming, and I can't fight it anymore. She agrees to chat with me again tomorrow. The moment my head lies on the pillow, unconsciousness swiftly pulls me under.

My alarm jolts me out of a delicious dream. My cock is throbbing from the thoughts I had about a woman I haven't even found the balls to ask to meet in person. Grabbing my phone as I go to the bathroom, I shoot off a few quick messages, the first to Hadley.

Connor

Good morning, a mhuirnín. I hope you had a
good, restful sleep.

Then, before putting my phone down, I remind my assistant to set up a meeting when everyone arrives for the day.

> Jordan, make sure that meeting is set for 8:30 .m. this morning so everyone can get started in the new capacity immediately.

Lastly, I send a quick message to my nephew.

> I'm not saying you were right. I'm also not saying you were wrong.

Stepping into the warm shower, I stand there for several moments, enjoying the hot water cascading down my body. My cock still hard, I wrap my hand around it, pumping myself. Images run through my mind of that gorgeous woman bent over in front of me as I plunge my cock inside her, my hand cracking against her ass as I thrust deep while gently teasing her clit. The thought of her coming around my hard dick has me ready to explode, the tingling sensation making its way up my spine just before I find my release.

Fuck, the way this woman has me wound up so tight...and I haven't even met her.

I stand in front of the engineering team, going over the projects we have now. With a number of new contracts signed and an increase in projects, I need to find a suitable project manager to take some of the workload, someone already established with the company.

"That being said, I would like to congratulate Mr. James on his promotion. He will be a project manager, overseeing the latest contract he has brought in for Quellin and Associates. I expect the team will have a lot of late nights in the near future, so if there is anything I can do to help, please let me know."

With that, I stand to leave while people meander over to congratulate Mr. James.

My day has been relatively productive, going in and out of meetings. I've messaged back and forth with Hadley a few times when I had a moment. I need to meet her, and soon.

I walk into my office to see my nephew, Sean, standing there.

"Howya, boyo!" I pull him into a hug. "What are you doing here? Don't you have classes until four?"

"Uncle, it's five o'clock."

He smiles at me like it should be obvious; I guess it should. This kid is too invested in his education to bail on classes.

"I had to see who had you texting me at four in the morning. Plus, you acknowledging that I'm right makes it so much better." His grin grows even wider.

I chuckle to myself as I hand my phone over. There is no point in denying the kid. Even at thirteen, I will forever see him as the eight-year-old boy I moved here to help my baby sister raise.

"Whoa, Uncle. She's beautiful," he says hesitantly.

I raise my eyebrow at him, waiting for him to continue.

"But..." He pauses. "She's married? That's a lot." He furrows his brow, showing his confusion.

"Usually, I'd agree with you, but something about her has drawn me in. I can't shake the need to know her," I respond.

My stomach is in knots. I know this could end in heartache, but damn. I have to try.

Chapter Four

I wake feeling so refreshed for the first time in a while. It has been a few days since I've seen Andy. Since he started dating Naomi, one of his coworkers, he has spent most nights with her. We have had maybe one Friday date night since our anniversary four months ago. It makes me nauseous thinking about it.

Today, though, I woke up with a new determination. I may have left my job to decrease stress so we could have a baby, but obviously that is low on Andy's priority list now. I miss teaching, and with our current relationship—or lack thereof—I decide to call a friend that just so happens to be a principal at Central Falls Elementary...and voilà! I am now Hadley James, substitute teacher extraordinaire. It won't be daily, but it's a start to return to my passion.

With Andy being less invested in our marriage at this point, I make the decision to get back on birth control too. My appointment is for later in the afternoon, so I spend my morning straightening up while listening to Avril Lavigne.

I'm belting out the words to "Complicated" when I get a notification on my phone. Checking it, I feel a smile spread across my face.

Connor:

> Good morning, a mhuirnín. I hope you had a good, restful sleep.

Hadley:

> Good morning, handsome! I actually did. I slept really well, and my morning has been highly productive. Even on only one cup of coffee. How was your night?

Connor:

> It wasn't bad. I couldn't stop thinking about you, though.

I am smiling at how sweet this man is when another text comes through.

I know this is pretty forward, but I'd love to take you to dinner this evening. Say seven p.m.?

My stomach flips in my chest. I have never been on a date with anyone but Andy. Can I do this?

I quickly tap the shortcut to FaceTime Ryan, my fingers trembling. She answers after two rings, her familiar face filling the screen. A moment later, Kat's worried expression pops up.

"What's wrong?" she asks quickly.

"You guys, Silver Fox just asked me out! TONIGHT!" I shout into the phone. "I can't do this." I sigh, burying my face in my hands.

Ryan chuckles. "Babe, you absolutely can. Have some fun. He is gorgeous, and you deserve to have some fun until Andy stops being a dumbass."

I can see Kat nodding in agreement next to her. "My love, I think it would be a disservice to yourself if you didn't. I mean, damn! Did you even look at his pictures?"

After taking a deep breath and saying our goodbyes, I've made my decision. I tap out another message.

OK, I'd love to. Where would you like to meet?

I make the mistake of texting Andy after my appointment, letting him know that I am going out with someone tonight. After all, we are supposed to be honest with each other for this to work the way he intended, right?

His response, though? Oh, it guts me all over again.

While I have no intention of sleeping with Connor right now, I am glad I've decided to start birth control again after that text. I really love Andy—I have for a freaking decade—but I'm beginning to question if he is the man I thought he was. His response to my date feels so eye-opening in ways I'm not prepared to unpack.

I stare at myself in the mirror for twenty minutes, unhappy with how I look. I have lost so much weight from the stress of this shitstorm that my clothes don't fit right anymore.

Fuck it. I can rock this, I tell myself with more confidence than I feel.

I zip up the red pleather knee-high boots and paint on some red lipstick to match. My slacks may not be as snug as I like them to fit, but I'm not going to let that stop me. The hem of the white cropped sweater I've decided to wear lands just below my breasts with a plunging neckline, making me feel sexy. My breasts have always been full, so even with the weight I lost, this top still looks amazing.

I make it halfway to the restaurant he chose, Visaggio's, before I start to panic and begin to second-guess my decision to go through with this. I know that Ryan was honest in my profile with my situation, and he is still interested anyway. Either he is a saint or just crazy.

Attempting to shake away my negative thoughts, I keep going. I am determined to see this through. Apparently, that's my mantra for the day.

I pull up to the valet and step out of my car, pausing to look around and see if Connor has arrived before handing the driver my keys. No sign of him.

"Phew. Okay, Hadley, just take a deep breath. You've got this," I whisper to myself, pulling in a steadying breath to calm my nerves.

That's when I notice the mouthwatering red Tesla Model S Plaid pull up next to me. My God, is it possible to be turned on by a car? Because, damn, it's beautiful. So beautiful, in fact, it nearly distracts me from the gorgeous specimen that emerges from the driver's seat. The instant our eyes meet, a panty-dropping smile covers his face and my brain short-circuits.

Oh. Dear.

"Hadley, a mhuirnín. You look even more breathtaking in person." His thick brogue sends a rush of heat to my core.

Oh. My. God. That accent is going to be my undoing.

Connor makes his way around the car, exposing his bespoke black suit bit by mouthwatering bit. Damn, that thing fits like a glove, each inch of black fabric tailored to his body perfectly. It's difficult not to notice, even from where I stand, that he is ridiculously fit. His arms are the size of my thighs, and he towers over my five-foot-six frame by at least a foot.

He turns to speak to the valet, giving me a peek at that glorious ass. Damn it, maybe I do want to sleep with him if this is where my mind is going already.

He approaches me hesitantly, a warm smile on his face. He leans in for an embrace, and I wrap my arms around his back for a brief moment, breathing in his intoxicating scent of sandalwood and lavender before releasing him. The contact feels nice, stirring up feelings deep inside my core that I haven't felt in months.

All from one little hug? Jeez, Hadley, get a hold of yourself.

"Connor, you are...wow. Yeah, your pictures don't do you justice either." I giggle, feeling heat rush across my face and chest.

Did I really just say that?

Chuckling, he responds, his words laced with desire. "Oh, a mhuirnín. Shall we?"

Placing a gentle hand on the small of my back, he leads me inside.

Well, shit.

Connor maneuvers me into a quiet room off the main dining area. Looking around, I take note of how private and romantic it feels. Wait, unless...oh, no. Nick and the Captain would be so disappointed in me.

"Are you going to kill me in here?" I blurt out, realizing I've probably listened to the *True Crime Garage* podcast one too many times after the words escape my lips.

A deep laugh bursts from his chest and a sinful smile plays on his lips. He raises a brow at me.

"What? Of course not. Why would you think that?"

"It's just that...the first time we meet, a private room?" I shake my head nervously. "Never mind. Don't mind me. I've just listened to one too many true crime podcasts," I ramble, twisting my hands in embarrassment.

Connor smiles down at me sweetly.

"Gorgeous, I just want to get to know you." His voice is gentle with that sinfully delicious brogue as he continues. "Without worrying that someone will come up to talk about business tonight. If you'd feel more comfortable, I will happily take you back to one of the tables in the main dining room."

Oh, heaven help me, I think as my heart melts.

Chapter Five

Connor

When I pulled up and saw her standing by the entrance, my heart nearly leaped out of my chest. I knew she was beautiful from the photos in her profile, but holy shite. She's lost quite a bit of weight since most of those were taken; however, she's still breathtaking. And the way she looks in that sweater should be illegal. My cock strained against the silk blend of my trousers, and I paused for a second to adjust myself before exiting the car.

Standing in the private dining room several moments later, Hadley wearing that worried expression, I attempt to assure her I honestly have no ulterior motive apart from avoiding people I know. Not because I want to hide her—I mean, fuck, look at her—but I just need some time to get to know her.

I stand nervously, second-guessing myself as she takes her time considering my offer of getting a table in the main room.

A sweet smile pulls at her lips as she shakes her head. "It's okay. I'm flattered that you want to give me your undivided attention."

"I'm glad, a mhuirnín. I know I said this already, but you are truly stunning."

I am finding it difficult to keep my hands to myself. This beautiful creature has taken all my attention. I gesture to a couch on the far end of the room, facing an already-burning fireplace. We walk over, my hand finding its way to her lower back yet again. As we settle in side-by-side, her subtle citrus and cinnamon scent has my cock twitching in my pants.

"Would you like a glass of wine? They have an opulent pinot noir they're very well known for."

A slight nod being the only confirmation I need, I pour us each a glass. I lean back against the plush couch, noting her lovely eyes watching me with curiosity and a hint of caution. My gaze meets hers when I decide I needed to know something I have no right to ask so soon.

"So, tell me something…"

"What do you want to know?" she asks shyly. Sitting back and getting comfortable, she crosses her legs, placing a lazy hand on her thigh as she sips her wine.

"Why would your husband ever want to give up having you to himself?"

She gasps at my brazen question.

"Tá brón orm, a mhuirnín. I'm thrilled to have a chance to get to know you. Just from our limited conversations, I can't imagine not holding on to you once you were mine."

She raises a brow at me teasingly. "I'm gonna need a glossary to keep up with the Irish vocabulary you're throwing out there."

"It means 'I'm sorry,'" I chuckle.

She stares into my eyes for a brief moment, letting out a soft sigh before responding. "Honestly? He said that he was unsatisfied that I was the only woman he had ever been with sexually. That he wanted to experience all that life has to offer." She lets out a huff. "Really, though, looking back over the last months since he made his declaration, I think he just wanted a pass to fuck his coworker."

Her eyes suddenly go round and she gasps, cupping her hand over her mouth like she can't believe she just said that aloud.

A strangled laugh makes its way out of my throat.

"Here I thought I was being direct," I joked as I place my hand over hers, still resting atop her thigh.

Fire licks my skin just from slight contact, and a heated look in her eyes tells me she feels it too.

"I'm sorry that he's hurting you. Selfishly, though, I am genuinely excited that you are allowing me a chance to get to know you."

We spend our time together chatting and sharing simple parts of ourselves: my favorite color, her favorite band. I tell her how my nephew created my profile when he came to my office while I was in a meeting and had left my phone on my desk. She shares with me how her friend Ryan did something similar. Never diving into anything too serious, our conversation flows pleasantly. As much as I want to dismantle the walls she's put up since her husband blew up her world, I know I need to move slowly and take my time.

We share a decadent meal made by Lorenzo, my close friend and the house chef. Before I moved from my home in Ireland, I had the displeasure of dining with his former employer, and I may have suggested to him that should he ever decide to leave the asshole he was working for at the time, I'd assist him in opening his own restaurant. He just happened to look me up when he learned I moved here to help my sister. Being an original investor provides its perks, such as this room.

"So, tell me something." Hadley's words echo mine from earlier.

Raising a brow, I gaze into her eyes and wait for her to continue.

"Don't look at me like that. It's giving me butterflies." She groans, realizing she said the words out loud.

I lightly brush my fingers across her cheek, feeling her quiver at my gentle touch.

"A mhuirnín, you have been stealing my breath since I saw your photos last night. I'll tell you…" I pause as I gather my thoughts. "My favorite is the image of you holding a coffee mug between your hands, sitting cross-legged on a couch. It looked like you were in a café, and you had the most fantastic smile on your face. You looked like you could conquer the world in that moment."

The way her face lights up at my declaration makes my half-hard cock throb in my trousers.

"What is it that you wanted to know, gorgeous?"

"I, uh…" Her cheeks are crimson, like she's still processing my words. "You mentioned your nephew signed you up for the app."

It's a statement, not a question. I can tell she's trying to formulate the thought.

"I'm just curious, as generous and kind as you are, why did he feel you needed it? I mean, look at you."

I chuckle at her response as my eyes roam over her. Has she seen herself? How the fuck her husband could want anyone but her is beyond belief. He must be out of his damn mind, but his stupidity is definitely my gain.

Chapter Six

H e laughs.

The beautiful man sitting next to me is laughing. At me.

God, I want to crawl inside myself. Never before have I been so nervous that my inner thoughts spewed out like that! It's as if I've lost all control around Connor, never mind all the sweet things he continued to say about my picture. It was taken during an afternoon out with Kat and Ryan. We had been having so much fun, and Ryan kept snapping photos of Kat and I with her new camera all morning to test out the settings.

That picture is one of my favorites. I look so carefree. I was much softer then too, my hips and thighs much fuller. I glance up at him while he continues to laugh. Is he disappointed that I'm not that same size anymore?

He chokes down the laugh abruptly. His large hand dwarfs my smaller one resting on my thigh as he gives it a firm squeeze.

"A mhuirnín, nothing about you could disappoint me. From what I've gathered in the short time we've been here chatting, this has been a stressful few months, and you haven't been taking care of yourself. That stops now, gorgeous."

Oh, my God. I said that out loud, didn't I?

He leans in and presses a gentle kiss against my temple.

"I don't know your husband, but I'm not going to sugarcoat shit. He's a motherfucking bodach for what he's said to you and how he's been treating you," he growls.

Connor takes a deep breath, pulling me into another embrace. I don't even bother trying to stop my arms from wrapping around him.

"Even if you choose never to see me again after tonight, a thaisce, I beg you to know your worth. You are so much more than what he's given you."

After a breath, he smirks at me, explaining the Irish phrase that had my brows furrowed in confusion. "It means 'lowlife.'"

I hold on to him, not quite ready to let go. A lone tear trails down my cheek while I look up into his beautiful eyes, the sincerity in his words spearing my heart.

"Kat and Ryan have been telling me that too," I tell him.

A gentle smile crosses his face as he leans in and presses his lips ever so lightly against mine. A gasp passes through my lips, and my hands move to the back of his neck. My fingers sink in, grabbing fistfuls to pull him in closer, deepening the kiss.

Lust and yearning bubble deep within my soul, my body vibrating with more need than I have felt in ages. I part my lips, welcoming his more experienced tongue to swirl and dive into my mouth. Chills erupt across my flesh as I savor the taste of him, moaning into his masterful mouth.

We pull ourselves apart a moment later, remembering that our private room is still part of a very public restaurant.

"That was unexpected," I whisper more to myself than to him, stealing a quick glance at his handsome face through my thick lashes.

"Unexpected, yes," Connor chuckles. "However it was also one of the most amazing moments I've experienced in my life."

He gently brushes a rogue strand of hair from my face, flashing me a devilish grin.

With a soft sigh, I smile up at him, wrapping my arms around his trim waist. "Tonight has been perfect. Thank you."

We continue chatting until the restaurant closes at midnight, getting lost in conversation so easily, it's like breathing.

As he stands, Connor holds his hand out to help me onto my feet as well. We walk to the exit and wait for the valet to bring our cars back around. Mine arrives first, and he leads me to the driver's side door, placing his hand so lightly on the small of my back, my knees nearly melt with the sexy gesture. I go to open my door, and he beats me to it.

Pulling the car door open, Connor dips his head and presses a chaste kiss against my lips. "Message me when you get home so I know you're safe, a mhuirnín."

With a gentle nod, that shy smile I've had so many times tonight pulls at my lips again. "I will. Goodnight, Connor."

I sent a message to Connor as soon as I got home and immediately passed out in a cute matching set of purple-and-peach-colored sleep shorts and a tank top.

Prying my eyes open at nine a.m., I'm aware of a noise in the near distance. As my brain slowly wakes up, I realize the noise is inside my house. I bolt upright, panic coursing through my veins.

My heart begins to beat a thunderous rhythm in my chest, the sound of my blood whooshing in my ears. What the hell do I do?

I grab my phone and start to dial 911 when Andy appears in the doorway of our bedroom.

"Oh, Jesus, Mary, Joseph and the camel!" I shriek. "You scared the shit out of me! What are you doing here?"

His eyes meet mine like I'm speaking a foreign language.

"What are you talking about? I live here," he replies, his annoyance palpable, like it should be obvious.

"Yes, well, you just haven't been home in so long, I wasn't sure you remembered where it was." I roll my eyes at him. "So, how's Naomi?"

I'm sincerely curious. I mean, after my date with Connor, I have no right to be upset anymore. Right?

"Don't be dramatic," he chastises. "I've been home at least one night a week when she's working late."

His long legs have him in front of me within only a couple of breaths. He presses a chaste kiss to my cheek, making my heart lurch in my chest.

I know I shouldn't compare, but him kissing me on the cheek feels so impersonal, whereas Connor's kiss lit me up like a firecracker.

Is Andy just trying to pacify me? Why, though, when I've already agreed to the open marriage? Hell, he began seeing Naomi almost as soon as the words left my mouth.

"Ah, yes, the one night a week I see my husband." I can't help the annoyance in my voice. "Speaking of, since tonight is Friday, will I see you later so we can have date night?"

I don't even attempt to hide my hopefulness.

"No." He doesn't even bother to give an excuse. "Didn't you have a *date* last night?" he snarks, saying the word *date* like it has air quotes around it.

Why is he acting this way?

"Uh, yes, I did. It was great, actually."

I smile at the memory of Connor's mouth against mine, his hand gripping my thigh over my hand. Damn, that was hot.

"Must not have been that great if you're still asking me about Friday date night," he responds coldly.

By this point, he has moved into our shared walk-in closet, adding more clothes to yet another suitcase.

"I've gotta go. I'll be home one night next week. You can make us dinner. I'll text you," he says dismissively, tossing the last bit over his shoulder.

And then he's gone. Again.

Suddenly, my phone pings with a notification, and my heart begins beating its way out of my chest. The small distraction is enough to shift my thoughts away from the pain I'm avoiding and thoughts of my marriage that I don't want to process.

Connor:

Good morning, a mhuirnín. I hope you had a good rest.

Hadley:

Good morning, handsome. I slept pretty well. Had a bit of a rude awakening, but I'm gonna make it a great day.

Connor:

Oh, a thaisce, if there is anything I can do to help make it a great day, I shall. Just say the word.

Connor:

Since we met last night, would you be open to exchanging numbers?

I smile to myself. I have never met anyone like him in my life.

Hadley:

That sounds good to me.

After a second message containing my cell number, I put my phone down to do a thorough deep cleaning of the kitchen. I pull on a pair of rubber gloves and fill a bucket with water and bleach. Before I dip the sponge in, I wonder how much bleach I'd need to use in order to trip up Lieutenant Kenda's team at a crime scene.

While my thoughts and emotions have calmed a bit just from the small message exchange with Connor, I still have some feelings to work through.

Chapter Seven

Connor

By the time I'm able to pick up my phone again, it's lunchtime. The team working on the Quellin Project has plans to work late, and I had planned to stay with them and even order dinner as a show of support for the team, but after re-reading Hadley's messages, I begin to second-guess my plans. I walk out to my assistant's desk to discuss the dinner plans for the group tonight.

"Hey, boss man. What can I do for you?" Jordan asks eagerly as I approach.

He's a good kid, sharply dressed and fresh out of college, hoping to work his way up the corporate ladder. He makes a great assistant, and I can definitely see him moving up in the company.

"Hi, Jordan. Would you mind finding out what everyone would like this evening? I was planning on staying and delivering dinner myself, but

I may have to leave earlier than I planned tonight." After handing him my American Express Black card, I turn back toward my desk.

Opening up my new favorite contact, A Mhuirnín, I press call and wait with bated breath for her to answer.

"Hello?" Hadley's voice comes on the line, soft and confused.

Fuck, I forgot to send her my number before I called.

Clearing my throat, I quickly reply, "A mhuirnín, it's Connor."

Even over the phone, I can hear the soft sigh of contentment escape her lips. I could listen to that sound forever.

"Oh, hello!" She sounds much more chipper. "I didn't expect a call. Usually, I don't answer numbers I don't know, but something told me I should." She giggles shyly. "Glad I listened to my gut."

Be still, my heart! This woman is everything.

"I'm sorry, gorgeous. I realized after I hit the call button that I didn't give you my number. I half-expected my call to get rejected. I'm so happy to hear your voice." I pause for a moment, contemplating if I'm moving too fast for her. "I was thinking, since you had a rough morning, I'd love to take you out again tonight. If you'd be interested, of course."

"I would love to, but Ryan and Kat are taking me to Ignite, the new night club that just opened last week." She sighs. "Would you like to have lunch tomorrow? I would like to see you again."

"Of course, a thaisce." I smile into the phone. "I'm glad your friends are going to make your day better. If you ladies drink too much, please call me. No matter the time. I just want to make sure you all get home safe."

"Thank you, Connor." I can hear the crack in her voice, like she isn't used to someone showing her they care.

Jesus, what is happening in this woman's life that she is unaccustomed to a simple gesture of kindness? Her husband must be a real arse.

"Well, I need to get a few things done before I get ready. I'll text you later, if that's okay?"

"I would be heartbroken if you didn't," I chuckle. "Have a wonderful night, a mhuirnín."

She disconnects the call before I pull my phone from my ear. The way I would like to tear her husband apart. He has effectively broken her. Putting my phone down, I go back to put my dinner order in with the rest of the team.

It's probably a good thing Hadley has plans. As much as I'd like to be the one to resolve whatever caused her earlier distress, I could use this extra time in the office to review proposals for how to expand our reach this year. The company has been growing with no problems. The tech industry is always growing, so long as you continue to grow with the industry. In a field where the only constant is change, it can sometimes be a struggle to stay relevant.

Around six p.m., I hear the ping of a text notification. When I pick up my phone, my lips twitch into yet another smile. Damn, I've been doing that a lot since the first message I received from her.

A Mhuirnín:

How does this look?

Attached is a selfie of Hadley through a full-length mirror. She's wearing a dangerously short skirt with another cropped sweater that sits just under the soft skin at the bottom of her breasts, showing a sliver of skin that has my heart racing. A pair of the sexiest red heels I have ever seen finishes off the outfit. I groan, my cock threatening to burst through my trousers. Images of those heels behind my neck with my face buried between her thighs, my tongue lapping up her arousal, flood my brain.

FUCK.

I glance down at my crotch. *Down, boy.*

It's gonna be a long night.

Mr. James walks into my office at midnight. "Hi, Mr. Quinn. I just wanted to let you know that we're all headed out for the evening. We've made some decent progress on how to continue with Quellin. We can continue next week."

His cell phone chimes in his hand, and with an annoyed glance, he silences it before putting it back in his pocket.

"Good enough. Have a good night, Mr. James." I wave him off as I finish rereading the same line in this document for the tenth time.

I groan, realizing that I've burned myself out. My phone vibrates on my desk, startling me. I rush to pick it up, worried something has happened with Sean. No one texts me this late unless there's an emergency. My nerves calm when I see Hadley's name on the screen.

"Howya, a mhuirnín. Did you have a good night?"

I can hear loud music thumping in the background, letting me know she is still at the club.

"Connor." She sounds deliriously happy to hear my voice. "I tried to get a ride, but he didn't answer," she slurs into the phone with an obvious pout on her lips, clearly several drinks in.

I can't stop the growl before it leaves my throat, but I manage to keep my tone even.

"Stay where you are. I'll be there in ten minutes. Do you need me to stay on the phone?" I ask as I grab my suit jacket and keys.

I walk toward the elevator and stab at the button to go down, anger slowly building inside my body.

"We're okay. We'll wait for you out front." Her voice quivers, and she sounds on the verge of tears.

Five minutes later, after ignoring every traffic law known to man, I arrive at Ignite. As promised, Hadley and two other women are sitting with her on the curb at the front of the nightclub. I barely get my Tesla parked before I jump out of the car, running toward her. I don't bother hiding the concern on my face when I get to the three friends.

"Are you all okay?" I ask as I round the car.

Hadley looks up at me through her long dark lashes, a heat flashing in her eyes that I only got a glimpse of last night. My cock instantly grows in my pants, straining against the zipper. Oh, Christ. She's more wasted than I thought.

In a single breath, Hadley is standing and jumping into my arms, her legs winding tightly around my waist. Her lips are on mine before I can even respond.

Damn, she's fast for being drunk.

I wrap my arms around her, accepting her tequila-flavored kisses. I groan into her mouth as she continues to grind her warmth against my already-hard cock. I gently pull away from her, breaking our kiss.

"Thanks for rescuing us," she slurs, reminding me that we are still in front of the very busy club with her friends.

Just kissing her set my brain into such a frenzy, I almost let the situation get out of hand—and in public, no less.

I gently set her down on the ground. "You don't need to thank me, a mhuirnín. I will keep you safe."

We turn, facing Hadley's friends as they cuddle one another on the sidewalk, their eyes trained on me.

"It's lovely to meet you. I'm Connor." I reach out both hands to assist them to their feet. "Let's get you ladies home."

I pull up to Ryan's house, stepping out of the car to make sure she and Kat get into the house okay. Hadley calls after us.

"Bye, Ry! Bye, Pickle! I'll talk to you tomorrow, babes!"

"Pickle?" I quirk a brow at Kat.

"I may be trashed, but I am not too trashed to take you out if you call me 'Pickle' again," she huffs.

Ryan laughs. "Don't worry. She likes the nickname."

Opening her door, she turns back to me.

"Take care of her," she says, momentarily looking stone-cold sober.

Just as quickly, she spins around, and with that, she and Kat disappear behind the door.

Hadley is asleep in the passenger seat of my Tesla within the few moments it takes me to get back to my car. Well, this isn't how I pictured taking her home with me.

We pull up to my long driveway, and I punch in the gate code before entering the secured grounds. I pull the Tesla into the four-car garage, coming to a stop next to my Harley Indian Challenger RR. I love this bike. Maybe I should take Hadley for a ride sometime.

Whoa! Slow down there, Connor. Let's focus on getting her in the house first.

Stepping out, I walk around the front of the Tesla to the passenger side, quietly opening the door and lifting Hadley into my arms. She lets out a breathy moan, and the sound does nothing to ease the tension in my pants.

I make my way inside to the master bedroom. Gently laying her on the bed, I contemplate for several moments before deciding to put her in one of my t-shirts for the night. It shouldn't make my heart flutter, caring for her in such an intimate way, having just met this woman. But the organ in my chest doesn't care how long I've known Hadley; it only seems to care that she's here in my arms. I don't know that I'd stop the intense reaction my body has to her even if I could.

After peeling her skirt down her gorgeous thighs, I gently replace her sweater with one of my plain black t-shirts. I chuckle quietly to myself; the shirt hangs on her small frame like a dress. I tuck her under the covers and slip in on the other side of the bed. As soon as my body hits the mattress, it's like an alarm goes off in her delicious body. She sits up and straddles me without saying a word. As she looks down at me, her lips twitch in a needy smile.

Fuck. Me.

I roll her onto her back, pinning her body to the bed. As I press my mouth to hers, my tongue licks along her bottom lip, gently asking for entrance. When she lets me in, my tongue caresses the warmth and softness of hers. I slide my fingers through her hair, grabbing a fistful at the base of her neck. With a gentle nip at her bottom lip, I slowly pull away, peppering kisses down her neck.

"Gorgeous, as much as I want you right now, I cannot take you this way. As soon as you are sober, we can revisit this, but for right now, I need you to sleep. I'm not going anywhere."

She lets out a strangled moan, as if ready to argue, but I roll off her onto my side, pulling her against me. Caged in my arms, she feels fucking perfect.

This. This is where she belongs.

Chapter Eight

I wake to a solid wall of warmth against my back and a strong arm holding me tight to a hard chest. I stretch before I open my eyes when suddenly the events of last night flash through my mind like a horror movie.

Not only did my husband not answer the phone, but the man I've only gone on one date with came to my rescue. And like the horny drunk I tend to be, I basically dry humped the man in front of the club.

My eyes fly open at the memories, my pulse quickening as the memories of my drunken state assault me.

Flushed with embarrassment, I move to look back at Connor, only to notice his arms are completely covered in the most beautiful and intricate Celtic knot tattoos. My mouth waters at just the sight of his strong, toned arms. His biceps are the size of my thighs, and that thought sends an aching need directly to my core. I hear the moan escape before I can stop the breathy noise from passing through my lips. Connor squeezes me tighter against his chest, obviously having heard the lust-filled sound.

"Good morning, a thaisce." His sleep-filled morning voice is gruff, making his accent even more prominent. It instantly turns my already-aching core into a molten mess.

"Good morning." I pause for a moment, embarrassment and shyness creeping in. "Thank you for last night. I'm sorry if I took you away from anything."

He growls into my neck. "You have nothing to apologize for. I'd be upset if you hadn't called me and had tried to make your way home yourself."

He rolls me onto my back, his morning wood pressing against my heat.

"How are you feeling?" he asks in a husky voice.

"I..." I choke as he presses harder, grinding against my already-drenched thong. "I feel better than I probably should," I confess, pressing against him, seeking out the friction I so desperately need.

"You had me aching last night." He smiles down at me, meeting me thrust for thrust.

His lips press against mine, urging me to open up to him, and his tongue begins a quick exploration of my mouth once again. Our tongues dance in a delicious tango that sends chills rushing through my body.

Fucking hell, I'm dry humping this silver fox all over again, and it's not enough.

Panting between moans, I breathe out, "You have me aching right now, Connor."

That's all the invitation he needs to run a finger along the damp, thin satin material of my thong. I buck up against his soft touch, needing more. He chuckles into me, his tongue still exploring my mouth. Connor slowly moves away from my pussy to hook a finger under the thin fabric, holding the material against my body before slowly, achingly peeling it away.

He pulls away from my lips; my chest heaves as I pant in need.

"Don't worry, gorgeous. You won't be aching for long."

He peppers kisses along my neck and chest, pulling his black t-shirt over my head and exposing my naked breasts to him. From the heat in his eyes, it appears Connor likes what he sees.

I feel so vulnerable, yet so empowered, like this. With his left arm holding him up, he hovers over my body. Using his other hand, Connor tenderly caresses my right breast while swirling delicious circles around my left nipple with his expert tongue. As he gently bites and pulls my nipples harder between his lips and teeth, I buck off the bed. Agonizing pleasure cascades over every nerve in my body, lighting it up like the Fourth of July.

I look down at my bare body to see him settling between my legs. Peppering light kisses against the delicate skin, he works his way north until his tongue is swiping at the apex of my thighs, eliciting an almost embarrassing groan from my mouth.

"Connor!" I beg, not recognizing my own lust-filled voice.

He chuckles again, this time right as his tongue slides the length of my slit. He laps up every drop of arousal he's caused since waking up, a low growl rumbling from deep in his chest.

Hell, who am I kidding? I've been aroused since the moment we met.

His tongue caresses my clit in a swift, but gentle swipe before he starts again on the other side. Teasing me back and forth before swirling around my clit, he presses his tongue firmly against my sensitive bundle, causing shockwaves of pleasure to jolt through me. My body begins to tremble uncontrollably as I writhe under his touch.

"Please, baby!" I scream, needing to come so badly I don't care if the neighbors hear me begging.

The teasing has me on the precipice and I just need to tip over the edge, headfirst into the coming ecstasy.

He pulls my clit between his lips, sucking hard, just as he inserts a thick finger inside my slick channel. When he instantly finds that sweet spot inside me, an explosion of euphoria courses through my veins. My gasps and sobs of pure bliss render me unintelligible for several moments as I come back down to earth.

"A mhuirnín."

I can hear the smile in his voice and against my thigh as he presses one last soft kiss to my clit before climbing up my body. He places his hand firmly against my throat and presses his lips to mine once again, urging me to open up to him. I part my lips, allowing him to devour my mouth as perfectly as before. I can taste myself on his tongue, making me moan into this kiss even more than the last one we shared.

Why is this so hot?

"Mm?" I mumble, not quite able to form a full sentence.

"You're still with me?" He smile against my neck.

"Uh-huh," I breathed.

Connor has moved to lie on his side, his arm bent at the elbow, his head propped on his hand. His fingers move from my throat, slowly trailing toward my breasts. Pulling a nipple between his thumb and forefinger, he pinches the hard peak, causing me to arch into his touch again. I let out a raspy moan, and his hand continues its exploration down my body. Finally reaching his destination, he cups my pussy.

"Gorgeous, I need to feel you come once more on my fingers," he says, parting my folds.

Connor's expert fingers toy with my clit, spreading my wetness before he thrusts a single finger inside my pussy again. After only a few thrusts, I feel him add another digit, stretching my tight hole in a delicious way.

"Oh, fuck!" I scream, my hips bowing from the bed to force him deeper. "Oh please," I gasp as he continues his sweet assault.

As I barrel toward my climax, he adds a third finger, and the sensational pleasure swirling in my lower belly from his touch has me at the edge.

"Oh. My. God!"

"Come, a thaisce." The words are gentle, but no less a command.

My orgasm hits like a tsunami. A gush of heat floods from between my thighs, and for a moment, I think that Connor came on my legs...until he begins lapping up the fresh wetness.

"Oh, gorgeous. You're a squirter? The fun I am going to have with you."

"I...what? I've never..." I stammer, looking at him in shock.

My brain is still buzzing from the intense orgasm, and I'm having a hard time understanding his words.

"You may not have before, but now that I know you can, I'm going to do my damnedest to make sure you come so hard you squirt a few times whenever we're together." He smiles devilishly. Peppering kisses back toward the apex of my thigh, he asks in a challenging tone, "Think you can handle another one?"

His tongue flicks against the ever-so-sensitive bundle of nerves again.

"I need to feel your cock inside me. I've been thinking about it since you had to adjust yourself behind your car the night we met."

The smile on my face is anything but shy this time. I feel like someone I don't even know, and I have to admit I like this Hadley.

"You noticed that, did you?" His gruff chuckle sends chills down my spine.

He reaches across my body to the bedside table, tugging open the drawer and returning half a moment later with a square foil wrapper.

I moan at the sight, not even realizing he lost his pants at some point. He fists his cock and tears the condom open with his teeth. Sheathing his impressive length all the way to the base, he gazes at me with a feral hunger.

"Oh, God. Please, baby. I need to feel you," I beg.

Before I can get another plea past my lips, the head of his dick begins to glide along the length of my pussy. He taps himself against my clit, the sensitive nub humming and ready for yet another earth-shattering orgasm.

Connor slowly enters me, just the crown of his dick breaching my entrance. Groaning into my neck, he continues to fill me with every inch, stretching me until he is fully seated inside my tight channel.

"Fuck, gorgeous!"

My body trembles with need as he allows me a moment to accommodate his generous size. He's so long and thick, and the curve to it! My God, he hasn't even moved, and I can feel him hitting that decadent spot deep inside me.

He slowly pulls out, then thrusts back in once, twice, three times before he picks up speed. With each pass, his beautiful cock slides against my G-spot, setting my body on fire. Each measured thrust becomes harder until he is fucking me at a steady pace that has me climbing the walls.

"Oh, my fucking God, baby!" I scream as my walls contract around his thick cock.

His punishing thrusts become erratic just as he follows me over the edge.

Chapter Nine

Connor

I collapse on top of her, my body covered in a light sheen of sweat.

"Holy shite," I breathe out, my chest rising in heavy pants.

I press a gentle kiss against her temple and roll to my side. Standing, I move to the bathroom to clean up and dispose of the condom. Grabbing a washcloth, I run it under some warm water before returning to my room. When I come back to the bed, I reach down to gently clean Hadley up, removing the evidence of her arousal.

After taking the washcloth back to the bathroom, I lie down and pull Hadley tightly in against me, her back flush to my chest.

"I don't have words for how amazing that was," she whispers shyly, tucking her face just out of sight.

We lie in silence for a while before she speaks again.

"I'm not sure what I'm supposed to do or feel right now." A sigh passes her lips. "On one hand, this has been the most amazing morning of my life, but on the other…it feels like I'm betraying him. Even though he's the one that wanted this. Even though he's doing the same with…with her."

"A mhuirnín, I won't pretend to know the dynamics of your relationship with him. This is the first time I've ever been involved with someone in an open relationship. While I will never understand how the hell he could want to be with anyone but you, I will not allow you to second-guess yourself." I press a gentle kiss against her temple. "Your feelings are valid. This morning has been one I will never forget, but if you need me to slow down, I can do that for you."

"That's the thing. I *don't* want to slow down. That's what scares me." She turns to me, a lone tear falling down her cheek. "I enjoy you." She giggles. "And not just your body. I enjoy being with you more than I thought I could."

She pauses briefly, a frown marring her perfect face.

"I've never come during sex before," she confesses quietly. "I've always had to get myself off in the shower after, and even then, it was never like that."

She blushes, her cheeks turning an adorable shade of pink.

"Oh, a mhuirnín. I will make it even better next time." A cocky grin spreads across my face as I internally high-five myself.

She's quiet for several moments before speaking again, her eyes locked on mine. "I don't want to walk away from this. From you."

Releasing the breath I was holding, I pin her back to the bed, my left hand holding her wrists above her head while I start grinding my already-stiffening cock against her pussy again.

"You truly are a thaisce."

She lets out a soft gasp just before I crush my mouth to hers, sharing a kiss with even more passion than before.

After spending the morning in bed, we both reluctantly leave the confines of my bedroom to rejoin the land of the living. When I hear Hadley's stomach grumbling, I make the decision that it's time for food for the both of us.

I send her to shower while I make a quick serving of my gran's beer mac & cheese. Nothing quite like comfort food after a hangover. The bacon she adds to the recipe is what really seals the deal for me. As I cook, I secretly hope Hadley will love this dish as much as I do.

By the time I've begun setting the table, Hadley strolls into the kitchen, dressed in another one of my t-shirts. Our height difference has it reaching her mid-thigh, her beautiful creamy skin on display as she enters. She walks toward me, a Cheshire grin spread across her stunning face. Wrapping her arms around my neck and stretching up on her tiptoes, she presses her lips against mine in a sweet, but heated kiss. My hands immediately reach for her ass, squeezing that perfectly-shaped peach. I pause for a moment when my fingers graze her bare lips and I realize she had no panties on.

"Gorgeous girl, you are going to be the death of me," I groan, pressing my lips against hers again. "Sit. Eat."

I reach down to adjust my rapidly-growing erection. I smirk at her, and she giggles, but does as she's told.

After she's fed and content, we migrate to the couch. I pull her into my side, wrapping my arm around her tiny frame.

Pressing a soft kiss to her temple, I let her settle into me before asking, "I hate to do this. Under normal circumstances, I'd have everything done before having you stay the night, but I need to check a few things with work. Do you mind If I do that while we sit here?"

"Oh, Connor, of course. I'm so sorry. If you need me to go, I don't mind." She sits up like she's ready to bolt.

"A mhuirnín," I growl, grasping her chin between my thumb and forefinger and lifting her gaze to mine. "That was not me trying to get rid of you. If you say no, I have no problem with that. I can catch up on Monday."

"Oh." She relaxes back into me. "Okay."

I reach over the arm of the couch to my computer bag and lift it onto my lap, pulling out my laptop. Hadley has herself snuggled up next to me, fully relaxed.

"While I finish this up, I do have something for you."

She looks up at me, and I grin down at her.

"I was planning on reading it so I could talk to you about it, but...." I let the words die on my tongue as I pull out a copy of *Finding Each Other* and hand it to her.

She turned to me, her cheeks tinged pink, tears pricking the corners of her eyes.

"You..." is all she manages before she presses her lips to mine for a brief moment. "Thank you." Her voice trembles as she tries to hide the sniffle.

Several hours later, once I've finished up, I place my laptop back in the bag and wrap my arms around her, pulling her closer to my chest. Hadley is so invested in the book, she doesn't even realize that I've stopped working. A wicked grin crosses my face as a thought forms in my dirty mind.

Shifting so I can kneel in front of her, I keep my eyes trained on her beautiful face. Even with my movement, her attention never wavers from the words on the page. Mildly impressed with her focus, I slowly part her legs. Still no reaction. Leaning closer between her legs to my new favorite place, I sweep my tongue up the length of her slit, twirling my tongue around her clit.

Hadley gasps, dropping the book on her chest. "Oh. My. God."

"Keep reading, a thaisce. I'm just enjoying a snack." I grin up at her as I devour her pussy.

I continue to lap at her clit in languid strokes until she grips my hair tightly in her small fist.

"Fuck!" she moans as she writhes under my touch.

Gliding a thick finger inside her, I slowly pump in and out of her soaking pussy, giving her a moment to adjust. She's so deliciously tight, and I can feel her squeezing me while I continue to tongue her clit. Adding another finger, I start grazing her G-spot slowly, with just enough pressure to have her on the brink.

"Connor! Please!"

Fuck, she begs so prettily.

I continue massaging her inner walls with a little more pressure and pull her clit between my lips, sucking hard. Her thighs clamp around my head like a vise as her climax slams into her. I hear her muffled screams through her thighs, my chest swelling with pride.

"Fuck, yes! Oh, my God! Connor!"

Her screams have my cock dripping. When I glance up from between her thighs, the most serene expression graces her beautiful face. She's always stunning, but seeing her high after a release is exquisite.

Chapter Ten

Connor and I have been together most nights since the night he rescued Kat, Ryan, and me. It's weird to say, but sometimes it's easy to imagine it's just him and I. Andy has been so far up Naomi's ass, he hasn't been home for weeks. I've tried to check in with him as we agreed, but maybe I'm naïve for thinking we can make this work.

The fact that he's only responded to one of my messages or calls speaks volumes about the state of our relationship. But after sharing so much of our lives together, I'm not prepared to say goodbye to him for good if we can fix this. No matter how strong my feelings for Connor may be.

It's been nearly a month that Connor and I have been seeing each other, and it has been a whirlwind. The fact that this kind man has become so ingrained into my life in such a short amount of time is both intoxicating and terrifying. I can't help but compare the two of them, which is so unfair. They're two entirely different people. One cares more for my needs than I ever have. The other, someone I expected to spend the rest of my life with, has become a stranger.

There once was a time when I thought Andy would do anything for me. Now I fear I've been hiding behind a veil of ignorance. There is no way he could have changed so much overnight, is there?

I've been subbing more frequently. Over the last week at the elementary school, I've only had one day off, which has been an amazing reintegration into the teaching community. I can't believe just how much I missed spending my days in the classroom, helping to enrich the kids' lives. It saddens me; I had hoped to have a child of my own or at least be pregnant by now.

That thought now seems so foreign. I mean, if I were to get pregnant, would Connor still want me? At his age, does he even want kids? I know he has helped to raise his nephew, but a child of his own?

Maybe I jumped too quickly into this. Maybe we're moving too fast. My thoughts sending me on a downward spiral is nothing new. Yet I'm more overwhelmed with each day that passes with my Irishman.

As if he knows I'm thinking of him, my phone pings with a message.

Connor:

A mhuirnín, I have a surprise for you tonight. Be ready to leave by seven. I'm having the wardrobe delivered to your place shortly.

Hadley:

What?! You don't need to get me anything to wear. I can run out and find something. I just need to know what I'm dressing for.

Connor:

That would ruin the surprise. (wink emoji) Besides, I got approval from Ryan and Pickle, so I know you'll love it.

Hadley:

Wait, what?

I get no response back. He's talking to Ryan and Kat? What the hell?

I send a video chat request to my girls. The ringing seems to take forever before they both appear on the screen.

"Hey, babes!" Ryan is way too cheerful, instantly putting me on guard. "What's up?"

"What's up? You tell me!" My voice has suddenly jumped three octaves, coming out as a high-pitched screech. "Since when are you two close enough to Connor to help him find me an outfit for some mystery date? And since when do you guys chat when I'm not around?"

I am talking so fast, I don't even know if they can understand me. I'm in the midst of a panic attack, and it's trying to pull me under.

"This is supposed to be casual. How can it be casual if he's getting so close to my best friends?"

I don't realize I'm shaking until I finally take a breath.

"Whoa, love. Breathe." Kat's soothing voice pulls me from the ledge. "Baby girl, are you back with us? Or do we need to come over for damage control?"

I half-laugh, half-sob. The snot coming from my nose is such an attractive sight, and I snag a tissue from the table beside me, attempting to clean up the mess that is my face.

"I honestly don't know. Also, when did he start calling you Pickle without fearing your wrath?" I sniffle.

"Ry dared him to when we were shopping for you. It's the accent. I didn't hate it." She laughs. "Now, do you want to discuss what just happened here?"

"I...I mean, I guess n—"

"I don't give a shit what you want right now, babes. You just scared the shit out of me. So we're gonna talk about it," Ryan cuts me off, and her *don't fuck with me* tone has me on high alert.

Shit.

"It's fine. Really, I'm—"

"No," she interrupts again. "We're not doing this. We love you, babes, so this is what's happening. He reached out to your friends to do something nice for you. Mind you, your actual husband has never, *ever* done this. Even when we were kids. It may have started out casual, but you don't do casual. Whether or not you want to admit it, you're in—"

"No. Don't you dare say that. I can't. Just because Andy wanted to open things up, I can't love two men. I just can't."

As I say the words, the argument sounds weak, even to my ears.

"Whatever, babe. Either way, this man adores the shit out of you. Enjoy whatever you wanna say this is."

"Baby girl...what Ryan is trying to say is even if you didn't mean for it to be more, it is. You don't need to admit that to us." Kat pauses. "But don't push him away. He's good for you. Also, Andy is a douche canoe. Have you even heard from him lately?"

I choke out a laugh at the harsh change in topic and sigh. "No. He stopped coming home at all a couple of weeks ago. I don't even know the last time he replied to a text or answered a call."

Kat doesn't say anything; Ryan looks like she's ready to hunt him down.

I know what they're thinking. I've been thinking about it too. Is my marriage over? Do I even care if it is anymore?

"You guys are gonna need to come over and help me get ready. How the hell am I supposed to know how to do my makeup or hair?"

Kat cackles. Actually cackles. "Oh, my love. We'll be there by five."

"I hate you both." I laugh.

By the time five o'clock gets here, I've had my head buried in a new book for the past two hours, my anxiety calming with each passing minute. I hear noise at my front door and stand just in time to see Kat and Ryan letting themselves in with a garment bag and shoebox.

"So you're the delivery service he spoke of?" I shake my head, chuckling, because of course they are.

The dress is absolutely phenomenal. I smile widely at Kat and Ryan. They really outdid themselves. I nearly faint when I realize it's a fucking Versace.

The black Medusa 95 midi cinches at my waist, giving me even more of an hourglass shape. The blue Medusa 95 strappy heels that they added complement the stunning garment perfectly.

Fuck, I feel sexy as hell the minute the fabric caresses my body. Since I've been with Connor, I've gained back some of my weight, my curves slowly coming back to life. He's always checking on me to make sure I eat. It's kind of adorable how much he cares and pays attention to such small things.

The doorbell rings at 6:59 p.m., and my mouth instantly forms a smile. This man refuses to be late, even when he has so much going on. Between work and making sure he sees Alannah and Sean at least once a week for dinner, his schedule is near bursting. I love that Connor is so close with his sister and nephew. He always makes sure to prioritize his family.

A bitter thought flits through my mind.

Would be nice if my husband prioritized our family.

As I shake the thought from my brain, Kat and Ryan go down to let Connor in while I grab my purse from my room. Taking a deep breath, I make my way down the stairs, holding onto the railing for dear life when I see him.

Jesus, Mary, Joseph, and the camel. The three-piece suit he's wearing fits him like a second skin. If I didn't know better, I would think it was painted on. His muscular arms fill the jacket out so well, I feel my knees buckling at the sight. And those trousers hug his thighs and ass so tightly I could bounce a quarter off them.

Where the hell did that come from?

"Jaysus Christ." His accent is so thick. "Mo stór. Tá tú foirfe."

Chapter Eleven

Connor

My heart flutters in my chest when Hadley makes her entrance on the staircase. The way that dress hugs her curves makes my mouth water. She looks exquisite. I can feel my already-fitted pants growing tighter across the front as I stare at her.

"You're drooling a bit, Connor." Ryan smirks at me.

"Shite, can you blame me? Mo stór. Tá tú foirfe," I repeat. "My treasure, you are perfect."

I reach out to grab Hadley's hand, helping her down the last steps. I pull her into an embrace, pressing my lips to hers in a chaste kiss. The moment quickly turns passionate as her mouth immediately parts, allowing me in. Our tongues dance in a fervor of longing, as if we have been apart for months, not mere days. Just as we start to get lost in one another, a throat clears somewhere behind us. We slowly pull apart, a beautiful pink tinge staining Hadley's cheeks.

"Okay, kids, go have fun. Have her home by eleven," Kat teases.

I chuckle, waving goodbye as I lead Hadley outside.

"Thanks, Ry! Pickle!" I call behind me.

I chuckle harder as I hear Kat groan at my use of her nickname.

I lead Hadley to the Tesla, opening the passenger door. Once she's safely inside, I close the door and walk to my side. Ryan and Kat told me how much Hadley loves dancing, even if she's awful at it. She hasn't let me see that side of her yet, so tonight, I've decided to take her to dinner followed by some dancing. Luckily, the country club I belong to has ballroom dancing on Friday nights.

Following the winding roads of the countryside, we ride in a comfortable silence, simply enjoying one another's company. Hadley reaches over, placing a hand on my thigh with a gentle squeeze; she smiles and glances over at me.

"I can't believe you did all of this." She motions down her body with her free hand. "Some days, I don't know what I ever did to deserve you. And don't get me started on how good you look in that suit. If you didn't have my curiosity so piqued with this surprise, I don't think we would have left my house." The coy words are dripping with desire.

I grip the steering wheel tighter so I don't swerve off the road.

"A mhuirnín." I let out a growl that sounds more like a groan. "You're killing me, gorgeous."

The giggle that passes her lips causes my heart rate to increase. I can't get enough of that sound.

I pull up to the valet and exit my car. Walking around to the passenger side, I open the door and hold my hand out to help her out. She takes a step in front of me, and I get a look at the back of her dress for the first time. I walk up beside her, placing my hand on the small of her back and lowering my lips to her ear.

"Jaysus Christ, you look like the most delicious kind of sin," I growl in appreciation. "And I'm damn well starving."

She turns to face me, her eyes meeting mine. We pause for a moment, both caught in the other's gaze, too afraid to say the words that seem just out of reach. The bright smile that takes over her face steals my breath. I lean down and press my lips to hers for a beat, but not deepening the kiss, knowing if I do, we will end up back at her place before the night truly gets started.

I place my hand on the small of her back again, guiding her to the entrance. Usually, I try to shy away from the public eye when we're out—not because I'm ashamed, but because I don't want interruptions. Tonight is going to be different.

As we pass through the doorway, it's as if a silent alarm goes off, alerting everyone that I'm here...and with a date. No one is used to seeing a woman on my arm when I come out, and that in and of itself is reason enough for me to anticipate garnering some sort of attention.

Out of the corner of my eye I see Ms. Phillips, an executive at Pacent Industries who has been trying to get in with DL for ages, making a beeline straight for me.

I can see the fire in her eyes as she gets closer, and I groan, pulling Hadley close. "Here we go."

"Connor!" Ms. Phillips greets with a saccharine smile. I watch as her gaze quickly flicks over to Hadley. "Who do we have here?"

"Ms. Phillips." I grin at Hadley, who has a sweet smile on her face. "This is my girlfriend, Hadley."

"Well, it's lovely to meet you. Maybe you can talk this man into working with my company." She winks at Hadley before looking back at me. "I would like another meeting to discuss contract options."

"We can discuss that during business hours. I only get so much time in the day with this gorgeous woman, which is never nearly enough. So, if you'll excuse us…" I tell her in a polite, but no-nonsense tone, motioning for Hadley to walk around her.

"It was nice meeting you, ma'am," Hadley calls out over her shoulder, waving goodbye before looking up at me. "Your girlfriend, huh? Just gonna go for it without asking a lady first?"

"Regardless of the title you want to go with, a thaisce, you are mine," I tell her, trying to let her see how serious I am.

"I like the way that makes me feel," she confesses, her face turning crimson with the admission.

I lean down to press a quick kiss against her temple. "Let's get to our table before anyone else comes up looking to talk business. I may love what I do, but I was serious. There will never be enough time with you, and I refuse to give up the precious moments that I do get."

Guiding her to a table in the far corner, I pull a chair out for her to sit, gently easing it back to the table when she is seated.

A live instrumental band is playing classical music on the platform next to the dance floor. After we finish our meal, I stand. Reaching my hand out for hers, I help her to her feet and lead her to the dance floor.

She turns to look up at me, a question in her eyes. "Uh, baby, what are you doing? I will make a fool of you out here!"

Ignoring her objections, I wrap her up in my arms, holding her close to me. It doesn't go unnoticed, though, that this is the first time she's called me "baby" outside of when we've been intimate. Pushing that to the back of my mind, I place one foot on the dance floor before she's trying to pull back.

"A thaisce, trust me?" I shoot her my most charming smile and see her reservations melt right before my eyes.

I twirl her around before she even realizes what's happening, and she's on the dance floor with me. With a lighthearted giggle, she relaxes against my chest. Holding her right hand delicately in my left while I place my other hand in the middle of her back, I lead her through a simple box step.

"The last time I actually tried to dance like this was at my wedding. The video proof that I saw the next day really just cemented that it was the vodka that had me thinking I could move." She laughs as she shakes her head.

"You seem to be moving pretty damn well right now." I slide my hand down to the small of her back, cinching her closer.

She gasps when she feels my stiff cock against her belly.

"The way you're swaying your ass to the music, following my lead, is so fucking sexy."

"Oh, my!" Hadley half-sighs and moans. "Take me home," she purrs. "Now."

We barely pass the threshold of her front door before our mouths are crashing together. Her lips part, her tongue passing into my mouth as she attempts to take control of the kiss. When I grip her hair and deepen the kiss, she moans into my mouth. Her hands roam under my suit jacket, gliding up my chest and peeling it off my broad shoulders, allowing it to drop unceremoniously to the floor. Her hands move back up to fist my hair, keeping my lips on hers.

I grip her hips, guiding her backward toward a wall while pressing my growing erection into her, our mouths still connected like a couple of teenagers making out for the first time. In a frenzy of need, she's fumbling button by button to get my waistcoat undone.

Gripping her ass in both hands, I lift her off the ground. Her legs instinctively wrap around my waist as I take the stairs, breaking the kiss for just a moment when we reach the top.

"Which room?" It comes out in needy pants.

She points to the right side of the hallway toward a room with an open door. Before I take even a step toward the room, our lips are fused together again, tongues tangled in a wildness that can't be tamed.

Once I enter the room, I pull away once, my chest heaving and Hadley panting heavily. Her lips are so swollen from our kissing, it makes my cock throb in my trousers. I nip at her lip and slide my tongue over the same spot, leading to the most exquisite sound I've ever heard pass another person's lips, half a moan and half a gasp that has me hard as steel. I toss her on the bed, startling her so much that she lets out a husky gasp.

I catch a glimpse of a wicked grin on her stunning face as I kneel in front of her. When I lift her dress to her waist, the reason for the grin makes itself known: she's bare underneath. Her pussy glistens with arousal, and I've barely touched her.

The groan escapes my lips before I can even stop myself. "Mo stór, had I known you had nothing on under this dress, I'd never have been able to leave here without tasting you earlier."

Gliding my hands up to cup her ass, I lift her up slightly right before I dip my head between her thighs, lightly running my tongue along the apex one languid stroke at a time. I press a soft kiss against her skin just above her clit, causing her to buck against my mouth.

"Oh, fuck, baby. Please!" She's begging, panting with need. "I've been drenched since you showed up in that delicious fucking suit."

I don't bother responding...at least not verbally. I drag my tongue along the lips of her pussy, gently nipping one side before moving to the other. Her moans are breathier the longer I tease her. Edging her, pushing her to that precipice, gets me even harder. It's nearly as exhilarating as the release itself when I'm finally inside her.

I swipe my tongue up the length of her slit, tasting her intoxicating sweetness, my new favorite flavor. I flick my tongue in slow strokes against her clit. The first swipe has her arching her back, grinding her pussy in my face. I chuckle against her skin, pressing her back down. I need to take my time with her tonight.

"Baby." She's barely audible. "I need you to make me come."

The declaration makes me growl as I feel my cock stiffening even more, straining against the front of my trousers. I'm so fucking hard, the damn zipper is going to leave its mark against my length. I glide my right hand from under her ass and slide a thick finger inside her slick channel, pumping slowly, allowing her to adjust to the intrusion she has been begging for. My tongue strokes her clit at a quicker pace as I slowly massage that sweet spot inside her. Her hips buck against my mouth; this time I allow her to find the rhythm she needs, matching it with my tongue stroke for stroke. Her moans become so loud they echo through the room, the sounds a symphony of desire and lust. I can feel her pussy start to constrict around the finger still massaging her inner wall, tightening so much my digit becomes stationary as she rides the wave of her orgasm.

"Connor! Connor! Oh, my God, Connor!" She screams my name in a prayer as she shatters around me.

It's the sweetest sound I've ever heard. I keep lapping her with my tongue, swirling around her clit until she comes back down from the orgasmic high. With one last soft kiss to the skin just above her clit, I rise, making my way up the length of her body to lie next to her on the bed.

"I... Oh... My. God." She's still panting, trying to catch her breath.

A sly grin spreads across my face. "Tá tú foirfe."

Chapter Twelve

I have never had an orgasm that intense before in my life. I stare at Connor in awe; this beautiful man is amazing in every sense of the word. And he's here, with me.

"You look like you're thinking way too much for how hard that orgasm hit you, a mhuirnín." His lips press softly against mine, my arousal still present.

I swipe my tongue across his lips to taste myself before he moves away. Why is that so hot?

"I was just thinking, I've never had an orgasm that intense before." I smile at the confidence I feel in the bedroom with him.

Connor doesn't just know how to please me; he genuinely seems to want to. I know I shouldn't compare them, but it's hard not to...

The cocky smile that spreads across his face makes my heart skip a beat.

"Stop looking at me like that!" I playfully smack his arm.

"Stop what? You just gave me the highest compliment, a thaisce. You can't expect me not to react." His cock twitches at that moment, as if it has a mind of its own.

I smile to myself as I rise to my knees. I lean over his chiseled chest, pressing a chaste kiss to his lips before dragging my tongue down the length of his chest, stopping every few inches to pepper kisses along where my tongue has already left a trail. I unbutton his slacks, sliding my fingers under the waistband of his pants and boxers. As I peel them down his hips and thick thighs, Connor raises himself enough for me to pull them off completely and throw them in a pile on the floor.

Gripping his thigh with my left hand and wrapping my right around his hard shaft, I swipe my tongue across the tip, which is already slick with anticipation. The salty, savory taste of his arousal has me moaning against him. I drag my tongue up the underside of his cock, teasing him until I reach his crown, where I swirl my tongue around, thoroughly enjoying what is now my new favorite flavor. I ever so slightly drag my teeth over his rock-hard length before I suck him deep into my mouth. The moan that slips past his lips sends delicious chills down to my core.

Inch by delectable inch, I suck him into my mouth until he's bumping the back of my throat. While I fuck him slowly with my mouth, my hand roams under to cup his balls, rolling them gently in my hand. He bucks his hips as I gently stroke my index finger against the sensitive skin just under his sack.

"FUCK YES, HADLEY!" he roars out in pleasure, his hands in my hair, holding my head in place as he thrusts into my mouth, fucking my face.

The harder he pumps into my throat, the more pressure I put into my strokes against that sweet spot that had him begging a moment ago. Once, twice, the third time sends him over the edge. The hot spurts fill my mouth, shooting down my throat as he shouts my name with his release.

I sit up on my knees, swiping my thumb across my lower lip, a wicked smile spreading across my face.

"My God, love." He looks down at me between his powerful thighs, his cock still hard even after the magical orgasm he just experienced.

The relaxed smile on his face is only there for a moment before a heated desire takes over once more. Before I have a chance to make another move, he sits up, grabbing my hips, and in a swift and seamless motion, he has me on my back. His lips crash against mine as I arch my back, pressing my breasts against his sculpted chest. My pebbled nipples brush against his flesh, alighting my skin with a burning need.

I moan, pulling away for a breath and fully ready to beg. "Bab—"

My plea is cut off by his hand slowly gliding up my ribs over the swell of my breasts. He takes a nipple between his fingers, rolling it with an exquisite amount of pressure. It causes just enough pain and sends shockwaves directly to my core.

"I need you so fucking bad right now, gorgeous," he growls.

Without saying a word, I reach behind my head to the box of condoms on the bedside table. I tear open the foil square and carefully pull the rolled latex from the wrapper with one hand, the other gripping Connor's length between us, slowly rolling it down and sheathing him to the hilt.

"What are you waiting for?" I tease as I wrap my legs around his waist, pulling him down to my entrance.

Fisting his hair with one hand, I use the other to slowly slide his cock between my slick folds, spreading my arousal and using the tip of his massive length to tease us both. He growls in frustration, causing me to giggle.

"Gorgeous," he warns, the word sounding feral on his lips.

His hand wraps around mine, still gripping his cock as he guides himself to find my opening, seating himself inside me with one forceful thrust. I gasp at the sudden fullness, but Connor allows me no time to adjust to his thickness, continuing to pump my pussy with languid strokes of his cock.

"Oh, God, please. I need more."

The wicked smile on his face causes my pussy to constrict, tightening around him so hard that he lets out a deep groan. Without warning, he begins fucking me faster and without reservation. The depth he is able to reach inside me is unlike anything I've ever experienced, and if I didn't know better, I would think he was rearranging my insides. My hips buck off the bed, meeting him thrust for thrust. The friction of his pelvis against my clit along with the fullness of him so deep has me ready to fall over the edge with another orgasm.

"I need you to come with me, baby. I'm about to see stars. I can't hold back."

"Fuck, Hadley." His voice is husky, the brogue thicker, making me ready to explode around him.

He must feel my walls tightening again because the thrusts become erratic before his command is my undoing.

"Come."

That one word, and I detonate, my vision darkening as my orgasm takes over in waves. I feel his cock throbbing inside me as he finds his own release. Knowing he has such control over my body is a heady feeling. He slides out of me gently, and after a quick trip to the bathroom to dispose of the condom, Connor returns with a washcloth for me.

We lie in each other's arms for several moments in a peaceful silence before he speaks.

"Earlier, at the club..." He pauses. "You called me baby. It was the first time you did that outside of the bedroom."

The warm smile on his face has my heart fluttering in my chest.

"You caught that, did you?" I smile at him.

"Indeed," the grin on his face is telling. "I love hearing you say my name, but when you refer to me as that term of endearment..." The heat returns to his eyes. "You could have me on my knees in an instant, mo ghrá."

Connor woke me at six a.m. to say good morning and goodbye. He had an eight a.m. meeting and had to leave way too early for me to function.

It's eight a.m. now, and I feel so deliciously sore, my body aching with the memory of our lovemaking. Since I have nothing planned for today, it gives me a reason to spend the day relaxing and reading.

After a quick shower, I make my way to the kitchen and start a pot of coffee. That rich aroma of the nectar of the gods fills my senses. Mouth watering at the glorious scent, I walk to the cabinet where we keep the coffee mugs. I pulled out my favorite *World's Best Boss* mug that reminds me of a time when Ryan and I used to watch *The Office* together religiously. A dull pain aches in my chest, and I sigh heavily.

I always thought Andy and I were endgame, like Jim and Pam, but it's feeling more and more like our storyline is ending.

With my first sip of coffee, the bitter liquid from heaven fills my soul with enough joy to make it through the rest of the day. The moment I sit down, my phone pings with a text notification. Groaning, I grab my phone from the coffee table, placing a coaster down before setting my mug on top. My annoyance at being delayed in drinking the nectar of the gods quickly evaporates the moment I see who the message is from.

Connor:

> Howya, a thaisce. Call me when you wake, gorgeous. Missing you already.

My heart skips a beat. Not bothering to respond, I press the call icon, listening to the ringing while I wait for him to answer. I pick up my mug and take another sip of my coffee.

"Mm," I moan as he answers.

"Howya, beautif—" He pauses. "Do I need to come back and help you take care of that?"

I nearly spit the coffee out of my mouth, choking on the liquid gold that I was starting to swallow when he answered.

"Oh, my God. Of course you would answer then. I was taking a sip of coffee!"

I snort and laugh simultaneously, causing a low chuckle to escape his lips.

"If you want to, though, I won't stop you," I purr.

"As much as I wish I could, a thaisce, I left my briefcase there when I left this morning. Is there any chance you can come by my office at lunch and bring it with you? We can go to the Thai restaurant around the corner for lunch."

"Of course, baby." I smile at the memory of the conversation last night. The pet name just feels right with him. "Just text me the address. I'll be there at one."

"Thank you, mo stór!" I can hear the grin in his voice.

We disconnect the call, and a text notification indicates he's already sent the address. With a smirk, I go back to my coffee and e-reader.

Thankfully, I've already showered, because by the time I look at the clock, it's eleven-thirty, giving me just enough time to do my makeup and get dressed. I decide to leave my hair down, letting my natural waves fall loosely down my back, and opt for a lavender long-sleeved cropped cashmere sweater showing off the softness of my stomach, a pair of black skinny jeans that hug my curves, and my Steve Madden stilettos.

I grab my purse and Connor's briefcase from my entryway and head to my car.

I pull up to the building a short time later and gasp, realizing where I am. Have we not discussed where he works? How am I just now realizing this?

Opening my car door, I climb out, standing on trembling legs. I walk toward the entrance with my phone in hand, texting Connor.

Hadley:

I'm walking into the lobby now.

Connor:

Jen knows that I'm expecting you. She'll bring you up to my office.

I take in my surroundings as I walk inside, noting how beautiful both the interior and exterior are. High ceilings, modern and clean lines. It looks like it's been remodeled slightly since I was last here. I wonder if that was Connor's doing?

Sure enough, I see a woman sitting at the reception desk. She looks up from her computer screen, noticing the case in my hand.

"Hadley?" she asks, grinning widely.

Smiling, I nod. "Yeah. That's me."

"Right this way." Jen bounces up from behind the desk, her cheeriness a bit overwhelming. She leads me to a set of elevators, which take us to the fifth floor, located on the top level.

The doors open to a beautiful open space, much like the lobby in the waiting area. It's breathtaking, but looks much more inviting than downstairs. A handful of oversized chairs fill the waiting room, facing the door where a young man sits behind a desk. He looks like he is straight out of college, his youthful face giving away his age. His disheveled, stylish blonde hair looks like he keeps running his fingers through it.

"Jordan, this is Hadley. Mr. Quinn asked that I bring her right in when she got here," Jen explains to the young man.

"Of course. It's so nice to meet you, Hadley! He's just finishing up with a meeting. Give me one moment." His genuine smile eases some of the anxiousness I was feeling.

Jordan stands and walks to the door off the left, behind his desk. With a light knock, he opens the door.

"She's here, sir," he murmurs politely.

"Thanks, Jordan." I hear Connor's deep voice from behind the door. "Thank you for the update. Keep me posted on the project status, alright?" His voice is getting closer.

Another voice I recognize is behind the door with him.

Oh, God. Please, not like this.

My pulse is suddenly hammering in my ears, and my breaths are coming in short bursts. This can't be happening.

The door opens, and sure enough, Andy and Connor emerge from the office. Andy stops dead in his tracks.

"What are you doing here?" His harsh tone is like a dagger, making me flinch.

I attempt to recover quickly, not wanting anyone to see the effect his words have on me.

"I'm here to see Connor, actually," I reply dryly, masking my hurt.

"Mo stór!" Connor walks past Andy, oblivious to the scene before him, and wraps his arms around me.

I melt into him without realizing it, finding instant comfort in his embrace.

"Mr. James, this is Hadley, my girlfriend."

"Yeah, I'm familiar," Andy snarls, shooting a dark glare my way. "She's my wife."

Well, shit.

Chapter Thirteen

Connor

"This is Andy?" I look at the man I've always referred to as Mr. James with a raised brow.

Hadley nods cautiously. "I didn't realize you worked at the same company until I pulled up here. I've only been here once, and Andy doesn't really share anything about work with me."

She's fighting to keep a mask in place, but I can see the wariness in her eyes. The bodach doesn't seem to fucking notice.

"Mo stór, it's okay." I give her a quick reassuring squeeze before releasing her from my embrace.

"So, this is the guy you told me about?" Mr. James—er, Andy—glares at her.

"Yes." Her voice is steady.

I didn't realize just how toxic their relationship was. Yeah, I know he started this open relationship bullshit, but had I known he was this much of a fucking bodach, I wouldn't have just been enjoying time with her. I would have made her mine. Only mine.

"Obviously, this is going to need to end. You can't continue fucking my boss—"

He doesn't get the chance to finish that shitty thought, and before I can stop myself, my hand is wrapped around his throat. I shove him back into my office against the wall, Hadley hot on my heels, a soft shriek at my outburst escaping her lips.

"You will *not* speak to her that way. I don't care if you are her husband or not. You haven't been around for a month. You haven't seen what your request has done to her," I grind out, my lip curling in disgust.

I'm not even shocked at the venomous snarl that is coloring my words.

"Furthermore, whether she and I have a relationship is up to us. Not you. Do. You. Understand. Me?"

I enunciate each word of the last sentence with a bit of added pressure to his throat, the words not a question so much as a statement. Because there is no question. Whether he likes it or not, until she tells me she can't be with me, I will not walk away. Maybe not even then.

After a weak nod of his head, I pull my hand from his throat, taking a step back to give myself some space.

Turning to Hadley, I pause, my voice coming out much calmer. "Tá brón orm. Are you okay, a mhuirnín?"

"Yes, I'm fine, baby." Her sweet smile tells me everything I need in this moment.

We're okay.

"Baby?" Andy scoffs.

The spark that ignites is palpable.

Hadley gives him a glare that would have me on my ass. "Andy, I love you, but I don't know who you've become over the last six months. What

I do know is that you are not the man I married. *You* are the one who wanted this. You are the one who said you needed 'a well-rounded life experience,' so I gave in. I said okay. Now that I'm seeing someone, you do not get to dictate who that person is. I didn't tell you not to sleep with Naomi. I've even tried to make conversation to see how that experience was going for you, but you've shut me out. So, quite honestly, I don't want to hear it."

I stand to the side, my eyes on Hadley and mouth agape. Holy shite, a fired-up Hadley is hot as fuck.

Her intense gaze softens when she meets mine. "Are we still on for lunch?"

"Yes, mo stór." I place my hand on the small of her back and lead her out of my office.

We enter the restaurant after a ten-minute walk through the city streets. She has been in her head the entire time. When we finally take a seat in the booth, I sit across from her.

"Are you truly okay?" My heart is aching waiting for the response.

"Honestly?" She shrugs. "I'm pissed off, but I'm not going to allow that to damper my time with you."

She grabs my hand across the table and squeezes gently, as though she's trying to convince us both that she's okay.

I don't bring it up again. We continue our lunch as though our relationship hasn't just been thrown in a fucking blender because of my job. Not to mention the fact that I absolutely assaulted one of my employees, and said employee is her fucking husband. That's going to look fantastic with HR, icing on the fucking cake.

"Would you like another drink, ma'am?" asks our waiter, who, in my opinion, has been entirely too friendly with her for my liking.

I glare up at the young man, who is completely oblivious. He's lost in that enchantment I know so well, the allure that is Hadley. However, my mantra plays on a loop.

She. Is. Mine.

It's on repeat in my mind. I know it's not necessarily the truth at the moment, but that's where my brain is currently living.

"We're fine," I interrupt before she can respond.

I'm being an overprotective prick right now, and I know it. I just don't care.

"I didn't know." Her soft declaration pulls me out of my own thoughts.

"You didn't know what?"

"If I had known you were his boss, I never would have let it get this far. I don't want to cause issues with his job. I don't want to be the reason you have an issue with him." She's rambling, wringing her hands in her lap nervously.

"If that's the case. I'm glad you didn't know." I pause, allowing my next words to sink in. "Even if you told me right now that you had to walk away from me for him, and let me be clear…" I stare deeply into her eyes, letting her see the sincerity in my words. "I really hope you don't. Even if you said those words, I wouldn't trade one moment I've shared with you. You are so special to me, mo ghrá."

I don't translate this time. Instead, I stand from my side of the table and slide in next to her, wrapping myself around her and pulling her close to my chest. We sit there for several moments before her phone pings with a notification. She pulls away just enough to look at her phone, but doesn't leave my embrace.

Andy:

> I'm sorry. You were right. Can we go to Providence? We haven't been out in weeks. I want to make things better with us.

She puts her phone away with a sad laugh and wraps her arms around my torso, holding on even tighter. It takes a few minutes before either of us is ready to let go.

When she pulls away from me, her eyes are red and glassy with unshed tears. "You mean so much to me. No matter what happens, I wouldn't trade a moment of our time together either."

Chapter Fourteen

A fter lunch, while we're walking back to Connor's office and my car, I send a text to Kat and Ryan asking them to come over. I need my girls to get my mind around the fresh hell that has happened today and what it could mean.

When we get back to his office, Connor walks me to my car, wrapping an arm around my waist, and pressing me against the driver side door. He leans down, crashing his lips against mine so possessively that my body melts into the sculpted contours of his chest. He breaks the kiss before I'm ready, and we're both panting with a need for more.

"Tease." I playfully smack his arm.

The lopsided grin that takes over his beautiful face turns my al-ready-heated core into a delicious molten mess. He takes a step backward and moves to open my door.

Pressing a quick kiss to my temple, he says, "I'll call you later, gor-geous."

Kat and Ryan are already at my place by the time I get there. I step out of my car, and Kat closes the distance between us, wrapping me in a tight embrace. I wrap my arms around her for a brief moment before releasing her.

"Are you okay, babe?" She shakes her head, as if answering her own question. "Obviously you're not okay, but are you as okay as you can be?"

I laugh. "I don't even know what to say. Connor and I never really discussed work because he would always get hounded by people if they saw him in public because of how exclusive the company is with the contracts it takes." I sigh. "I respected that boundary and didn't ask questions. It's not like I got a crime boss vibe from him."

Ryan shoots me a curious look. "I mean, he *is* Irish. What if he's in the Irish mafia?"

Kat and I's eyes meet, and we both fall into a fit of giggles.

"No, not even close," Kat responds before I can. "Girl, we went shopping with him and he does not give off mafia vibes. Possessive alpha, sure, but there is no way he's mafia."

I snort out another giggle, nodding my agreement. "If he was, I don't think that's something he could hide with as much as we have been together since we met."

"Whatever. I'm not crossing it off my list of possibilities." Ryan crosses her arms.

"How many mafia romance books are you currently reading?" I smirk at her.

"That's not even relevant." She rolls her eyes, obviously annoyed with us. "I'm not here to be judged. I'm here for you. So spill."

They follow me into the kitchen to grab glasses and ice for the whiskey they brought, and we sit around my kitchen island. Pouring a hefty portion, I lift the glass to my lips, taking several swigs before I describe the events of the day. While I find their shocked expressions amusing, it doesn't overshadow the confusion I have at what unfolded this afternoon.

After several moments of silence while they digest what I've shared with them, Kat speaks first.

"Babes, I will never forgive Andy for how he's treated you in doing this. However, you won't forgive yourself if you don't give him a chance to try to fix it." Her features soften as she speaks.

"I don't like it, but Pickle is right," Ryan says as she raises the glass of whiskey to her mouth, letting out a soft moan of appreciation as the dark liquid passes her lips.

I lift my nearly-empty glass from the table, taking a sip before I let out a groan. "You're both right, and I hate it. I wasn't supposed to care for Connor like this."

With a sympathetic nod of encouragement from both of my friends, I pick up my phone and tap out a response to Andy's previous message.

Hadley:

We can go to dinner on Friday. I'm not happy with our situation right now, but the only way for us to try to fix it is to actually spend time together.

Andy:

Thank you for giving us a chance. I love you, Had.

I don't respond to his text. I do love him, but I don't know if that's enough anymore.

As I press my hand to my chest, my heart aches and my insides are twisted up like vines. It's going to take a hell of a lot more than whiskey to numb the emotions swirling around inside me.

Connor and I have been speaking every day and have spent most evenings together since we found out Andy was one of his employees. Thankfully, Andy hasn't gone to HR or caused any issues after the confrontation in Connor's office.

Now that Friday has finally arrived and I know I'm not going to see him at any point today, I feel the anxiety building. Unease fills my chest, not only because I'm not going to see Connor, but because I *am* going to see Andy. His texts have been sporadic at best over the past week, but more than he's sent since this all started.

I do want our marriage to work. I just don't know what that looks like for me now.

I spend an entire hour picking out clothes, and my bedroom floor looks like a tornado hit by the time I decide on a simple teal scoop-neck midi dress. It's form-fitting, showing off the soft curves I've finally gotten back, and has me feeling like my old self again. I pair the dress with my black leather boots, giving me an extra three inches. My hair is styled in loose waves, lying across my shoulders and down my back.

After a total of two and a half hours since I started the process, I swipe my lashes with one last coat of mascara, and I'm finally ready.

I'm in the kitchen, having a glass of wine to calm my nerves, when the front door opens at exactly seven p.m. Not used to having anyone just walk in, it startles me, and I scream.

Andy comes running in the room.

"Are you okay?" Concern is etched across his face.

"Oh, God. You scared the shit out of me." I feel my face heating, my hand on my chest. "I'm not used to anyone just walking in anymore. Not that you shouldn't be able to just walk into your own house."

Shaking his head, he smiles at me. He takes a hesitant step forward and wraps his arms around me in an awkward hug. He pulls back enough to tuck a strand of my long hair behind my ear, leaning in to press a sweet kiss against my lips.

My mind is whirling. I don't know what I expected to happen tonight, but if the rest of the evening continues this way, it's going to be a good night.

We chat for a little bit while he catches me up about work and I tell him about my substituting position. He seems happy that I decided to go back to work. He doesn't bring up Connor, and I'm hesitant to bring up Naomi. When the clock marks seven-thirty p.m., we head out toward our cars. I had intended to drive myself. Considering he hasn't been staying at our house for so long, I don't expect him to tonight.

When I pull my keys out of my purse, Andy gently grips my wrist. "Don't be silly, Had. I'll drive."

I just nod, not quite sure what to say. Does this mean he's going to stay with me tonight?

Unsure how I feel about the thought, I walk toward the passenger side of his sedan and let myself in. It smells strongly of lavender, and looking around, I see evidence of Naomi all over: ponytail holders, a jacket, a floral gym bag.

My stomach lurches, acid crawling up my throat. He's been playing house with this woman.

I try to shake that thought from my mind as he climbs into the driver's seat and starts the car. The ten-minute drive to the restaurant goes by in a blur. When we pull up, I see Jim's bright smile as soon as he notices us arrive. My heart lightens the moment I spot him.

"Well, this is a wonderful surprise, sweet girl." He comes in for a quick embrace. "I've missed seeing you *two* together. I was starting to worry."

The way he says the word "two" makes me think Jim is trying to tell me something.

"I've missed you, Jim!" My cheerful greeting is always genuine with him. This man will forever hold a special place in my heart.

We spend a little time catching up with Jim, and I notice Andy on his phone the entire time. While I am annoyed that he's on his phone, I'm usually the one talking Jim's ear off. Jim and I say our goodbyes before Andy and I head inside, Andy clearly distracted by the device in his hand.

We've been sitting at our table inside Providence for forty-five minutes. I'm already on my second glass of wine. He's paid more attention to his phone than he has to me, and honestly, I feel like I had more of a conversation with Jim on the way in than I have had with Andy.

"So, how's work been? I haven't talked to you in so long." I place my hand on his to get his attention, a soft smile on my lips when he looks at me.

"It's been fine. I got a promotion a while ago. No big deal." His response is short.

He smiles down at his phone, and alarm bells start going off in my head.

"Who are you texting?" I ask apprehensively.

"None of your fucking business!" he snaps at me.

I pull my hand away with a quickness I didn't realize I was capable of.

"Oh." Shocked, I don't speak any more for several moments, picking up the glass of water I haven't yet touched.

I chug the water to try to sober up before I say something I can't take back. I pull out my phone and send a text asking for a ride and a place to stay. Not that I think he'll go back to our house, but honestly, I don't want to see him anymore tonight.

Hey, I'm sorry to bother you. I know you had plans tonight, but if you can, can you pick me up from Providence, and can I stay with you tonight?

I wait for several minutes for a response, still sitting there just staring down at my hands, while my husband—who I haven't seen in over a month and have barely spoken to—continues to ignore me for his phone.

I'll be there in ten minutes, a mhuirnín.

I breathe a sigh of relief. I'm not sure where the man I married went, but he sure as hell isn't the same man sitting across from me. Without saying a word, I stand from my chair. Andy doesn't even look up from his phone as I pick up my purse and walk toward the door.

Jim is standing there when I come out. He walks over to me, seeing the devastation written on my face.

"Oh, sweet girl, what happened?"

My resolve shatters as soon as his arms wrap around me. This sweet man has been more compassionate than my own husband tonight, and that fact hurts more than it should, especially after the treatment I've been receiving from him for the last month. I don't bother holding in my sobs anymore. Feeling safe in Jim's embrace, I let it all out.

"He brought her here, didn't he?" I sob into Jim's chest.

"Yes." He doesn't say anything more.

I have so many questions, but I can't find the strength to ask. And even if I did, what good would it do other than to break my heart more?

The Tesla arrives so quietly that I hear the door open before I realize it's even there. I'm still holding on to the comfort Jim is providing when suddenly, I feel Connor's hand on my shoulder.

"Mo stór," he whispers.

The brogue washes over me like a blanket of comfort. I slowly release Jim and look up at him.

"Take me home," I sniffle as I wrap my arms around his waist, squeezing him in an embrace. "Please."

I look back to Jim and offer a weak smile before walking toward the car with Connor.

The drive is silent; I'm not quite sure what to say. I asked my boyfriend, who happens to be my husband's boss, to rescue me from a date so awful beyond words with my husband. To his credit, Connor must sense that I'm not ready to speak, his only form of communication being his large hand on my thigh. He gives me a gentle squeeze every few minutes, his silent way of letting me know he's here.

I'm so in love with this man, and it's terrifying me. I shouldn't be this far gone with someone who wasn't supposed to be serious. That was the deal I made with myself, wasn't it?

Chapter Fifteen

Connor

I was with Alannah when I received the text message from Hadley. I was dreading tonight all week, and Alannah told me to come over for dinner. We had just finished eating when my phone dinged with the message. The moment I read those words, my stomach dropped.

A Mhuirnín:

> Hey, I'm sorry to bother you. I know you had plans tonight, but if you can, can you pick me up from Providence, and can I stay with you tonight?

I see her standing with her head on an older man's chest, shoulders shaking with sobs. I've never wanted to simultaneously hold someone in comfort while wanting to obliterate someone else like I do right now. My pulse thumps with my growing rage. Not at Hadley, but at that bodach. How could he do this to her? I may not have expected this, but I've fallen so madly in love with this woman. I will do whatever it takes to make her mine and only mine.

I pull up to my house once the gate opens and park in the garage. I let myself out of the driver's side before walking around to Hadley, opening the door and holding my hand out for her to stand. Taking her hand, I lead her inside, making it to the kitchen before I turn to her.

"Did you have dinner?" I ask, giving her a stern look.

I know for a fact she has a habit of not eating when she's upset. I refuse to see those luscious curves wither away because he's upset her yet again.

"No, but I'm not really hungry." She gives me a small smile. "I had a few glasses of wine and then drank my weight in water in case I needed to walk home when I decided I needed to leave."

"Fine," I concede. "But if your stomach growls, you're getting mac & cheese." I give her a look that says *I dare you to argue.*

"Thank you, baby."

She raises on her tiptoes, wrapping her arms around my neck, fisting the hair at the nape to pull me closer. She presses her mouth to mine, her tongue swiping at my bottom lip, urging me to open to her. I part my lips, giving her the illusion of control, as if I'm allowing her in. Before she has a chance to react, I slip my tongue into her mouth, taking over. As I deepen the kiss, my hands slide down to cup her ass and lift her into my arms. I step toward the closest wall and pin her against it. Her legs instinctively wrap around my waist, and she tugs my hair, trying to keep me close. I pull back for a breath.

"What do you need, mo ghrá?" I bend to press my lips against her neck, swiping my tongue across her pulse. I nip at the sensitive flesh, knowing she won't be able to hold back an audible response.

"You, baby." She throws her head back and gasps. "I. Fucking. Need. You." She pants each syllable, a darkness present in her eyes I've not seen before tonight.

She looks like she wants to be fucked into oblivion.

"How fond of this dress are you?" I smirk at her.

The gleam in her eyes tells me all I need to know. I carefully place her on her feet, keeping her pinned against the wall. My hands travel up her hips and over her soft curves, one hand cupping her breast, teasing her pebbled nipples through the fabric. My other hand travels further to her neck, gripping with just the right amount of pressure to hear the involuntary gasp leave her mouth. My grin widens as I take her in.

"You. Are. Mine," I growl, the words sounding almost animalistic.

The hand that was on her breast moves to the scoop of the dress she's wearing. My fingers glide down and, grabbing the fabric with both hands, I tear it from her breathtaking body, revealing her bare chest and the worst excuse for panties I've ever seen. The tiniest strips of lace and elastic to ever exist barely cover her, and the sight of them sets my body on fire. Dropping to my knees, I slide my tongue along the length of her slit, flicking at her sensitive nub through the thin material, causing a moan to pass her lips.

"Yes. Yours," she breathes just as I tear the panties from her with my teeth.

Still on my knees, I lift her legs onto my shoulders, burying my face in her luscious cunt. I lap at her swollen clit in languid strokes as she arches her hips toward me, grinding her pussy onto my face, seeking more. I slide a hand underneath her, pressing a thick finger inside her opening as she rides my face. The moans become shouts of pleasure as she quickly finds her release, my face covered with the proof of her climax. I lower her legs back to the ground and stand in front of her again, a smirk pulling at my mouth when I see her legs trembling. When I press my lips to hers, she deepens the kiss, taking me in, our tongues swirling together. She moans into me the second she tastes the evidence of herself on my tongue.

Hadley's hands move in a rush to my slacks. My belt is unbuckled, trousers unbuttoned, and the zipper lowered before I have a chance to catch my breath. Breaking the kiss, I watch her as she pushes the slacks down my hips onto the floor like they've personally offended her. I chuckle, stepping out of them.

Cupping her ass, I lift her into my arms, her toned legs wrapping around my waist once again. I start walking toward the bedroom, needing to be in her *now*. Her eyes haven't left mine, and I can tell she's thinking hard about something.

Bet I can help to clear her mind, I think smugly.

I make it to the bed, tossing her gently and enjoying the sight of her perky tits bouncing. I go to grab a condom when she grabs my wrist.

"I haven't been with anyone but you since this started. I'm clean and I'm on birth control." She pauses. "We don't need to use them, if you don't want to."

The shyness in her voice has my cock throbbing.

"Mo ghrá," is all I can say before I walk back to her, the box of condoms forgotten.

I climb on top of her, crashing my lips against hers once again. No more words are needed in this moment. The thought of taking her bare has me nearly coming right now, my cock dripping in anticipation. I position myself between her legs, pressing a kiss against the spot on her neck that drives her wild. Planning on taking it slowly, knowing I will likely embarrass myself if I take her right now, I slide my hand down her body, feeling the smooth softness of her curves. She's groaning in frustration under me.

"What is it, beautiful?"

"I need you to fuck me. Please, baby. I need to feel you fill me up."

FUCK.

"As you wish, mo ghrá." I line myself at her entrance, gripping her calves and holding her up at the perfect angle.

I guide myself in, filling her to the hilt with one quick thrust. Her cunt is slick with arousal, and she lets out a delicious gasp.

I groan loudly at the decadent feeling. "Tá tú foirfe."

I slowly pull out before thrusting hard, the head of my cock hitting deep inside her.

"Fuck, Connor! Yes, God, don't stop!" The sweet pleas coming from her lips do nothing to hold me off.

Dropping one of her legs, I move my hand to her glistening slit. My fingers find her pulsing clit, massaging in firm circles, urging her to fall over the edge so I can follow. It happens so quickly, and as her orgasm takes hold, her delicious pussy tightens around my cock and she screams out her release.

My name is a prayer on her lips. "Oh Connor, Connor, oh Connor."

The feeling of her release along with the sound of my name coming from her lips has me losing any control I have left. With one last thrust, I erupt inside her, filling her with my seed and giving her everything she begged for.

Thoughts of my weekend with Hadley run through my mind on Monday morning, a cocky smile playing on my lips. I hop in the elevator at work, my brain using the short ride to picture all the positions I put Hadley in and how much I loved hearing her scream my name.

I exit the elevator only to find Mr. James—well, I guess Andy—waiting for me. He looks like he hasn't slept for a few nights. I know I haven't, but my lack of sleep has been more enjoyable than what it looks like he's been dealing with.

"Can I talk to you?" he asks as he follows me to my office.

"How may I help you, Mr. James?" I ask in an attempt to maintain some degree of professionalism.

"Cut the *Mr. James* crap, Connor. Have you seen my wife? She disappeared on Friday night, and I haven't heard from or seen her since." He's glaring at me, and the accusation in his tone pisses me off.

"I have. She's fine. If she wants to speak with you, she'll call you. I'm not playing middleman for you, Mr. James." I keep the annoyance out of my voice, keeping my mask of civility firmly in place. "While we may have a connection outside of this building, it will not be discussed within these walls. Understood?"

"Whatever." He hangs his head and turns to leave, his defeated response pleasing me.

I pull out my phone to send a quick message to Hadley. She went home this morning after spending the entire weekend with me. My cock throbs in my pants at the memories of each surface we christened in my house. Unable to get enough of each other, we fucked everywhere, and now that we have no barriers between us... I will never have my fill of her.

Connor:

I miss you already, Mo Ghrá

A Mhuirnín:

I miss you too, baby. I wish I could stay with you tonight, but I got called in for work tomorrow.

Connor:

It's alright, beautiful. I will just have to leave work early tomorrow to make up for the time missed tonight.

A Mhuirnín:

I like the sound of that.

I debate for a moment telling her about Andy's visit. Deciding I don't want him to blindside her, I shoot off another text.

Connor:

Andy stopped by my office today asking if I had seen you. He said you've been missing since Friday. He knows I've seen you. Just keep an eye out, mo ghrá.

I need to get back to work. I'll call you later, beautiful.

A Mhuirnín:

Thank you for letting me know, baby. I'll talk to you soon.

Chapter Sixteen

Coming home on Monday morning was surreal. My body was deliciously sore from the workout Connor gave me over the weekend.

Now I'm in the home I share with my husband. But do I really share it with him anymore? I haven't heard anything from Andy since I left him at Providence on Friday. When Connor told me he came to him, I actually snorted. Who does he think he is, acting like the victim now? Annoyance and anger flicker just below the surface, making me wish I knew what he's thinking.

What is his plan here? Does he really care where I am?

Tuesday has come and gone in a flash. I love spending the day with the kids; they're all so smart, and it fills my heart to be a part of their learning. Even though I'm only subbing for now, it still feels like I'm making a small difference. Pride fills my chest as I think about how much I love being in the classroom, and I'm so grateful I was able to go back into teaching.

Walking out of the school, I see some stragglers on the playground. I wave at the kids and their parents as I make my way to my car. I've texted Connor on each break, but unfortunately, we kept missing each other. I miss him so much, and I'm looking forward to seeing him tonight.

My phone rings as soon as I get buckled in my seat. I smile when I see his name and press the green accept button to take the call.

"Hey, baby! I've missed you today!"

"Mo ghrá, it's so good to hear your voice." His voice is gruff.

"Babe, what's wrong?"

"It's just been a day. We've had some contract issues. Nothing I can't take care of." He's silent for a moment.

"If you need to cancel tonight, it's okay," I reassure him.

I may hate that I haven't been with him in twenty-four hours, but I know his job is pretty damn important.

"I'm so sorry, love. I don't want to." The frustration is apparent in his voice.

"Baby, really, it's okay. I'll call Kat and Ryan and hang out with them tonight."

"I'll make this up to you, I promise."

I smile at his declaration.

"Call me when you make it home?" he asks. "No matter the time."

"Of course. I'll talk to you later, baby."

"Mo ghrá."

I haven't figured that one out yet, but he also hasn't translated. I'm too nervous to ask.

We hang up, and I send out a message in the group text.

At that, I smile. I've missed them too. Even if the orgasms are unbelievable, I need my best friends too. It's been way too long since we've had a girls' night.

Two hours later, the three of us are sitting around a table at our favorite dive bar, Finley's. The table is cluttered with every appetizer on the menu and our second round of drinks.

I'm mid-sip of my screwdriver when Kat announces, "I think I'm going to sleep with Clay."

Ryan and I share a knowing look.

"The owner of your gym, Clay?" Ryan's question is filled with amusement.

"Yep. He's been hinting that he wants to take me out for months and, well, I think I'm going to sleep with him," Kat declares confidently.

"It's about damn time, woman!" Ryan and I say at the same time.

She looks back at us, startled.

"Seriously? Am I that obvious?" Her tone is light with amusement.

"Listen, babes, Had and I have been waiting for you to take the plunge for a while. He's a good place to start." Ryan pauses thoughtfully. "I know Anya fucked you up, but it's been a long-ass time for you to not be interested in anyone. If you're attracted to him, get that dick, Pickle!" Her voice rises with her growing excitement.

Kat is mortified, her face a bright shade of crimson I've never seen outside of Saturday morning cartoons.

"On that note, I think we've had enough to drink." I giggle and grab the check the server laid on our table a few moments ago, pulling out my credit card to pay the bill.

I walk out to the parking lot with Kat and Ryan, and we stand by our cars and chat for a little longer. Once the three of us get together, it's difficult to separate us. These girls are the sisters I always wanted.

Eventually, we say our goodbyes, and I climb into my car. Thankfully the drive home is short. I park in the driveway, pulling out my phone before I open the door to send a quick message to Connor.

Hadley:

I just got home, baby.

I put my phone away, not expecting a response immediately with how stressed he sounded earlier, then step out of my car and walk toward the door.

I go to put the key in the lock when I realize the light is on inside. I didn't leave that on, did I?

Not thinking any more of it, I push my key in the lock and turn it, letting myself in. I step inside, locking the door behind me. I take a few steps into the foyer when I hear music coming from the kitchen.

What the fuck?

Fear courses through my body, and I grab the first thing I can find, an umbrella which was left on the entryway table. Taking the last few cautious steps into the kitchen, I feel like I've stepped back in time.

"Hey, Had." Andy's voice snaps me back to reality.

"Why are you here?" The question is out before I can stop it.

"I miss you. I thought I'd stay home for a bit." He smiles at me, but I can see the mask he's trying to hide behind. "So, where were you tonight?"

"None of your fucking business." I spit his words back to him from Friday night, my fear having disappeared and anger now taking its place.

He sighs. "I know that was unnecessary. I'm just under a lot of pressure."

Hesitantly, I sit at the bar. "It was more than unnecessary. It was cruel. How long did it take before you even realized I left?"

He deflects my question, setting me on edge. "I figure the only way for us to get back to the same place we were would be if I started staying home more. So, here I am."

I stare at him, dumbfounded. I did want this at one point, didn't I?

"I don't know that I want you here after how you treated me. How you've *been* treating me," I reply, trying to force some bravado into my tone that I sure as hell don't feel.

"Of course you do. I'm your husband." The gleam in his eye frightens me.

I walk away, going up to the room I stayed in with Connor. We were never together in the master, because even with all the shit Andy has pulled, it still felt disrespectful to my marriage. At this moment, I am thankful I made that decision. I don't want to sleep next to him. I don't even want to be in the same room as him. Having this space that I shared with Connor makes me feel safe. I lock the door behind me and pull my phone out of my back pocket, opening the text app and sending two texts, the first to Connor.

Hadley:

> Hey, baby. Call me when you can. Not urgent. I just need to hear your voice.

I add a kissing emoji before pressing send. The next text goes to the group chat.

Hadley:

> *My night went from joyful buzz to WTF. I came home to Andy in the kitchen declaring he will be staying here to "repair our relationship."*

The response from the group chat is instant.

Kat:

> What in the actual fuck?

Ryan:

> Jesus, Pickle, I didn't think that you had that in you. What the hell though, Had? Are you OK?

Hadley:

> I don't know. I'm staying in the spare room. I don't know what to think. He's not who he was when we got married anymore. If he's willing to try, though, shouldn't I?

The texting is interrupted by an incoming call. I can't help but smile when I see his name. I press the accept button and bring the phone to my ear.

"Hey, baby."

"Mo stór, what's going on?" His voice is laced with concern.

"Well…" I let out a sigh. "Andy was here when I got home. Apparently, he's staying here to repair our relationship."

"Oh." The defeat in his voice breaks my heart. "Is that what you want?"

"I don't know," I admit. "I'm sleeping in the spare room. I'm not ready to share a bed with him." I pause for a moment. "If you need to walk away, Connor, I understand."

"Oh, beautiful," he growls. "I don't care if you're married. You. Are. Mine."

He enunciates the last three words to ensure there is no mistake in his meaning. It sends intoxicating chills through my body.

"Am I going to see you tomorrow night?" I change the subject to try to lighten the mood.

"I'll be there at five. Stay the night with me?" he asks, his voice husky.

"I'd love to." I smile brightly at nothing but my inner thoughts. "How late are you working tonight, babe?"

"A few more hours, unfortunately, or I'd come get you now." He lets out a strained sigh, and I can hear the frustration in his voice. "I miss you, beautiful. Get some rest. I'll check in with you in the morning."

"Goodnight."

I change into one of Connor's t-shirts I stole this weekend. Pulling the collar to my face, I inhale deeply. It still smells like him. I climb back into bed and snap a selfie of myself in his shirt, a playful grin spread across my face. I open my text app to send one last message along with the picture before I crash.

Hadley:

I miss you. Can't wait till tomorrow.

Putting the phone on the nightstand, I fall asleep just as a reply comes through.

I wake up with a jolt, hearing a commotion downstairs. I unlock the bedroom door and creep downstairs to find Andy and Naomi yelling in the foyer.

"Do you really think you can go back to fucking just her?" she snarls at him.

"Damn it, Naomi! Keep your voice down. She's sleeping."

But his attempt to quiet her is an epic fail. She notices me over his shoulder, a glare taking over her otherwise pretty face. She wraps her arms around his neck and pulls him in for a kiss, an obvious power play on her part. At first, he tries to push her away, but I watch as he falls further into the kiss, my stomach roiling at the scene before me. I clear my throat, and he quickly pushes her away.

"Had, it's not what it looks like." The desperation makes his voice sound shriller as it echoes toward me through the open floorplan of our home. "I told you, we're over. I want to make things better with us."

"You don't have to stop on my account. You wanted to open the marriage. It's open. I'm not ending things with Connor. You do what you want." I walk past them to the kitchen for some coffee, my head held high.

I hear him grumble something at her and the front door slams shut. Heavy footsteps sound in the hall getting closer to me.

"What do you mean, you're not ending things with Connor?" he snarls. "Of course you are. We're fixing this. You're my wife."

I roll my eyes as I pour my coffee and turn to go back to the spare room to avoid him. It's too early to deal with him this morning.

"Andy, *you* are the one who wanted to find someone to have a 'full life experience' with, so *you* can deal with the fact that I'm enjoying that 'full life experience' as well. God knows I've had to deal with you *experiencing* things with Naomi for the last few months."

"Get the fuck back here, Hadley. We're not done." His voice is low, the rage rolling off him like waves.

Instead of acknowledging him, I simply continue back to the spare room and drink my coffee, pride filling my chest at having stood up for what I wanted. I check the message from Connor telling me he's counting the moments until I'm in his arms, which just makes me swoon harder. I send a quick response before I go into the group chat and text back and forth with Kat and Ryan for a bit, letting them know what's going on and trying to determine my next move. My phone lights up with a response instantly.

Ryan:

> **Well, babes, what do YOU want?**

I take a deep breath as I read the message.

What do *I want?*

Chapter Seventeen

Connor

My eyes fly open to the sound of water running.

What the fuck? I sit up quickly and look around, double-checking my surroundings. I am in fact in my own bed, in my own house.

Damn. I thought maybe I had fallen asleep at Hadley's, but no such luck. I jump out of bed, going in search of the running water. Like the first victim of a horror movie that goes to investigate a strange noise in the basement, I creep through my house looking for an intruder. Maybe I should have grabbed a bat from my closet. Well, too late now, I suppose. Rounding the corner to my kitchen, I come to a screeching halt when I find my baby sister, Alannah, and my nephew, Sean, making breakfast.

I immediately relax and send up a silent prayer, thankful that I fell asleep in my gray sweats now that I realize I'm not alone. Alannah's back is toward me, and she's cooking something that smells a lot like bacon on the stove, her bright red hair tied in a messy knot on top of her head. Sean's doing dishes at the sink.

Ah, so that's where the running water was coming from.

I clear my throat before speaking. "You could have called first, sister."

The startled sound that comes from her petite frame amuses me. "You just scared the shite out of me, brother!"

She's clutching her chest like I'm the one that was in her house when she woke up. I chuckle, shaking my head at her.

"Boyo!" I greet Sean.

I walk to him at the sink and give him a quick hug before crossing to Alannah, pressing a kiss to her head.

"So, to what do I owe the pleasure of the two of you making me breakfast?" I ask with a raised brow.

"You don't recall texting me at three a.m. because Hadley's husband moved back in?" Alannah's tone is laced with worry.

"Ah, that." I attempt to mask my emotions, not that I really can with Alannah. "I'm fine. We're still seeing each other. It's just going to be an adjustment."

I realize at the mention of seeing her that I left my phone in my room.

"Before you crack on, give me a moment."

I walk back to my room, my hands scrubbing my face. Alannah is as protective of me as I am of her. This is going to be a deadly chat. I grab my phone from my bedside table and see a notification from Hadley.

A Mhuirnín:

Good morning, baby. I can't wait to be in your arms too. I didn't sleep well without you last night. What time are we meeting tonight?

I smile to myself as I step back into the kitchen with my phone in hand, tapping out a reply before putting my phone in my pocket.

Connor:

I'm working from home today, beautiful. Come over anytime.

Alannah and Sean are at my dining room table with places set. The fresh coffee at my chair is calling my name; however, the stern look on my sister's face tells me she's unimpressed with the smile on mine.

"Boyo, take your plate to the den and give us a moment." Alannah's voice is full of annoyance.

Sean and I share a look before I nod for him to go. Alannah waits until he's out of earshot to begin her lecture.

"You are setting a terrible example for him doing this, Connor." The exasperation is even more unmistakable. "He's going to think it's okay to break up a family."

I hold up my hands, telling her to stop. "Sean is much more intelligent than you're giving him credit for." I take a sip of coffee before continuing. "He asked me if it was a good idea. If she was just cheating on her husband, yes, that would make me an arse, but her husband is the one who asked her to open their relationship."

I give her a moment, allowing the information to sink in when my phone dings.

"I really hope you'll give her a chance before you condemn what's going on with us," I say as I pull the device from my pocket.

A Mhuirnín:

Is now OK? I can get a shower and leave here in thirty minutes.

A lopsided grin crosses my face, and I see Alannah roll her eyes at me.

"Of course I'll give her a chance. If she hurts you, though, Con, all bets are off."

"Good, because she'll be here within the hour." I take a bite of a strip of bacon on my plate. "This is really good, sis." I wink at her.

"You're unbelievable," she snickers. "Boyo!" she hollers to Sean, who comes walking out with an empty plate a moment later. "Help yourself to some more. Uncle is expecting company he'd like us to meet."

Sean refills his plate without a word, yet a knowing smile plays on his face.

The three of us continue enjoying our meal while Sean tells us about his schooling. He declares he's decided to go to college for architecture. His grades are good enough that he can go to nearly any school he sets his sights on. My heart swells with pride at how far this kid has come since I moved here. Both of them have been through so much, yet they've been shining brightly for a while now.

Alannah tells me about the construction company she works for and how they've been looking to sell. The owners are older and don't have any kids to leave it to. Naturally, she's worried about what that will mean for her and if she'll get to keep her job. I offer encouragement and a job if all else fails, which she smacks me upside the head for. The doorbell rings, and before I can move, Alannah is on her feet crossing the length of the house to the front door with incredible speed.

The door opens, and I hear Hadley's voice.

"Oh. Hi. Um...is Connor here?"

Alannah's gentle laugh and muffled response has me on my feet, walking toward the door as quickly as possible. I reach the door as Alannah is moving to the side, allowing Hadley to enter.

Alannah turns back, smiling at me. "Don't worry, brother. I was just introducing myself to your girlfriend." She turns back to Hadley and motions for her to walk inside. "Come, we still have plenty of breakfast."

Chapter Eighteen

Hadley

I t takes about sixty seconds before the door opens when I ring the doorbell. I'm startled by a beautiful redheaded woman standing in front of me. Her hair is piled high on her head, and her slender body is so tiny compared to my soft curves. She smiles warmly at me as she greets me.

"Hello?"

The question in her voice is making me nervous. I've never seen anything indicating a female spent much time here.

"Oh. Hi. Um..." I stammer. "Is Connor here?"

The smile brightens as she responds to me quietly. "Of course. Hadley, right? Come on in. I'm Alannah. It's lovely to meet you."

She steps aside, and I see Connor looking from the far end of the hall, his jaw clenched, almost like I just walked in on something. It only lasts for a second until I'm walking toward him.

"Hi. It's so nice to meet you too," I say shyly, crossing the hall.

A devastating smile takes over his face and he meets me in two steps, wrapping his arms around my waist and pulling me to his chiseled chest. He presses his lips to mine with such passion, my knees nearly buckle. I push on his chest when I remember we're not alone. He groans against my mouth, and I giggle.

"I've missed you too, handsome."

"You have no idea, beautiful," he says, not releasing his hold until Alannah clears her throat.

"Brother, let the girl breathe," she laughs while stepping past us.

We follow her into the kitchen, where I see a young man sitting at the table with a plate piled high with pancakes and bacon. His bright red hair matches Alannah's. This must be Sean. Connor's hand on the small of my back leads me to a chair near the head of the table, where an empty plate awaits.

"Hadley, this is my son, Sean. Sean, this is Hadley. Please, Hadley, help yourself," Alannah explains.

Taking my seat, I smile at Sean. "Hello. It's so nice to meet you. Your uncle has told me so much about you."

The grin that spreads across Alannah's face warms my heart. I place a small helping of eggs and bacon on my plate, and Connor raises his brow at me. I roll my eyes at him.

"I wasn't expecting breakfast. I stopped by Mud House for coffee on my way here and had a croissant on my drive over. I promise I'm eating plenty." I place my hand on his, which is resting on the table.

With a nod, he continues his meal, and the four of us fall into an easy conversation. Sean is so animated when talking about his aspirations for school and college, and it's easy to see the pride both Alannah and Connor have in their eyes when they watch him speak. Once we finish, Alannah stands to do the dishes, and I follow her.

"I'm really glad I was able to meet you today. Connor talks so much about you both," I share while she washes and I dry.

She's quiet for a moment.

"It's been nice meeting you too." After a pregnant pause, she continues. "I know your situation is very unique. My brother hasn't had a relationship with anyone since he moved here to help me. So, for him to take such an intense liking to you so quickly... I have to admit, it worries me."

"I have no intention of hurting him. I care about him so much." My reply is quiet. "I hate the situation I'm in. Part of me wishes I had met Connor first."

We share a look, and she nods her head before we continue washing dishes in silence.

I'm sitting on the couch next to Connor, my legs in his lap as he's working on his laptop, and I'm nearly done with *Finding Our Way*, the sequel to my favorite book that was just released a week ago. I hadn't even mentioned it to Connor, yet he had it sitting on the coffee table when I sat down. The temptation to drop to my knees and take him in my mouth while he was working was so strong when I saw it. Unfortunately for both of us, he's got meetings over Zoom, and as much as I want to thank him, I'm waiting until the distraction won't be caught on camera.

By the time I've finished my book, Connor has finally ended his last Zoom call of the day. He puts his laptop on the coffee table and stands to stretch, his muscular arms extending above his head, causing his t-shirt to ride up, giving me a nice peak at his toned torso. God, he looks beautiful. He turns to me, as if ready to say something, but before he can get the words out, I do what I've been waiting all morning to do.

Dropping to my knees, I hook my fingers under the waistband of his gray sweatpants, which are doing nothing to hide the outline of his already semi-hard cock. I tug the pants down over his hips, releasing his dick, then wrap my hands around his thick thighs and grin up at him, sliding my hand to grip his length before kissing the tip. I swipe my tongue across the head to taste the arousal that's been waiting for me, wrapping my lips around the crown and sucking gently when he speaks.

"Beautiful," he groans. "I don't know what I did to—"

His words are cut off by a moan as I suck him to the back of my throat, not allowing any time for myself to adjust to his size. I gag slightly, but recover, swallowing him as deep as I can. My need to bring this beautiful, thoughtful man pleasure is overwhelming. The delectable groans of pure bliss that escape his lips send heat to my core. I pull him out to the tip, gently running my teeth over the crown, which results in the sexiest, most primal moan I've ever been the cause of.

"Fuck, mo stór." The words are barely audible.

His control fails at that moment, and his hands move to my hair, grabbing fistfuls as he holds my head still and fucks my mouth with no hesitation. Hot tears roll down my cheeks as he takes what he needs. Gripping his left thigh, I move my right hand to cup his balls, rolling them in my hand and finding the spot that made him go wild last time. I gently massage his perineum again, this time with more confidence, knowing the pressure that set him off, before I work my way up, thrust after thrust.

With one last violent plunge into my throat, he exclaims, "FUCK, HADLEY! Tá tú foirfe, mo ghrá."

Then he fills my mouth with his flavorful release.

I wake up wrapped in a cocoon of warmth. As I stretch my exquisitely sore muscles, a soft sigh passes my lips, and Connor stirs behind me.

"Morning, baby." I roll back to face him and press a soft kiss against the corner of his mouth.

His eyes are still closed, but he pulls me tighter against him.

"Morning, mo ghrá." His rough morning voice and thick brogue when he first wakes send a flood between my legs, which we have no time to take care of.

He presses his lips against mine, a kiss filled with so much desire I melt into him. His tongue passes my lips, plunging into my mouth to tangle with mine. I moan into his mouth as he continues taking what he wants.

Panting, I pull away briefly. "Baby, we both have to leave in thirty minutes."

He groans against my neck, the vibrations against my skin doing nothing to settle the growing need between my thighs.

"I will make it up to you tonight, beautiful." He kisses my temple before rolling out of bed.

"I promised the girls I'd go to dinner with them tonight. They're worried about everything going on at home. I have work for the next few days too." I sigh disappointedly.

"Well, then I may need to reschedule this meeting." He climbs back over me once he reaches the other side of the bed.

I squeal with laughter. "Babe, no. You've been waiting for Mr. Asher to take a meeting with you for a few weeks. You have to take it. Besides, if I get ready now, I'll have time to run to Mud House for coffee and breakfast on my way to work."

"Alright." He smirks when he slaps my ass as I crawl out from under him and stand up from the bed.

I make it out of Connor's in record time, arriving at Mud House as they're opening. Since I have extra time, I decide to have my croissant and coffee at a table inside. It's my first time stepping inside since it's been open. It's the third location of a local coffee shop in Grove City, only twenty-five minutes from Central Falls. Their coffee is so good, and their pastries are to die for.

I step up to the counter when I notice a large moose painting hanging on the wall to the left of the register. What the hell does a moose have to do with coffee? We're not in Alaska.

"Hello there! What can I get started for you today?" a beautiful, petite redhead with the greenest eyes I've ever seen asks me.

I'm taken aback for a moment by her beauty. I've never seen her when I come through the drive-thru.

"Oh, hi. Um, may I get a peppermint mocha latte and a white choco-late pumpkin croissant?" I smile at her, and she giggles.

"That's my husband's favorite too. I'll have it ready for you in a moment."

"Hey, can I ask you something?" I peek behind me, but there is no one waiting, so I might as well make small talk.

"Sure?"

"What's with the moose?" The curiosity is killing me now.

Her grin resembles the Cheshire Cat; it's so big. "When my husband and I first started dating, my son was only five and couldn't say monogamous, so he said mono-moose. It's been a running joke in our family since. Liam painted a moose for each Mud House so I can see it at any given location to remind me of my moose."

Chapter Nineteen

Connor

I received a call from Liam Asher ten minutes after Hadley left, asking me to meet him at his wife's coffee shop, Mud House. I smirk at the possibility of seeing Hadley again before going to the office as I grab my briefcase and make my way to my car.

The drive to Mud House is easy with it being so early and no traffic on the roads. Hadley's car is still here, and my face splits into a wide grin. I pull into a spot next to her; stepping out of my car, I grab my briefcase and walk inside, finding Hadley at the counter in a deep conversation about a moose. What in the world?

I walk up behind her and wrap my arms around her waist. Hadley screams for a second, but relaxes quickly when she realizes it's me. The redhead behind the counter smiles up at me.

"Oh, my God, baby, you scared the shit out of me." Hadley spins in my arms, whacking my chest. "What are you doing here? Aren't you going to be late?"

"Liam called, asking me to meet him here. Apparently, his wife owns the place. It's just a happy coincidence that I get to see you again, mo ghrá." I press my lips against hers.

"Mr. Quinn?" a deep voice interrupts.

I look up and see Liam Asher walking toward me from behind the counter.

"Liam, please call me Connor. This is my girlfriend, Hadley."

I don't miss how she melts into me when I call her mine.

"Of course, Connor. Hadley, it's a pleasure to meet you." He holds his hand out to take hers.

Without missing a beat, she extends her hand, shaking his firmly.

"It's so nice to meet you." She smiles brightly at Liam.

"Cap, your coffee's up," the redhead behind the counter calls in our direction, and a lopsided grin takes over Liam's face.

He walks back to the counter and takes the coffee, pulling the petite woman into his arms.

"Cap?" Hadley's the first to ask.

"That's a story for another time," he laughs.

Hadley excuses herself not long after to get to work, and Liam and I get down to business. I have ideas for a marketing campaign that his company can help DL Technologies Inc. with, helping us to grow even more this year.

We chat for quite a while about the ideas for marketing and our personal lives. He and his wife, Kayleigh, had a hell of a beginning. It makes me feel more secure in how Hadley and I are starting out. At least neither of us have a damn stalker.

Once I arrive at the office, I have to put out fires with several server issues that arise with high-profile client contracts. To say the day has been hectic is an understatement. Andy has been throwing me an attitude all week, and HR is starting to take notice. It will be a shite show when this comes to a head.

When the issues are finally under control, I finish my day with meeting after meeting. It's not until seven p.m. that I can finally check my phone. It's been buzzing in my pocket all damn day.

Alannah:

> She really is lovely, brother. I get it. Just be careful.

A Mhuirnín:

> The extra few moments today were such a good surprise.

Sean:

> I like her, Uncle.

The last one has a toothy grin splitting my face again.

A Mhuirnín:

> I can't believe how damn much I miss you already. I'll call you after dinner.

I pack up my briefcase and laptop for the day so I can get home before Hadley calls me. What I wouldn't give to have her in my arms tonight. With my phone in hand and key fob in my pocket, I head to my car. Once I get in and start the car, I dial Alannah. She picks up after two rings.

"Brother," she answers.

"So, you like her?"

I know she can hear the smile in my voice when she scoffs in response.

"You never could resist gloating. Go ahead, say 'I told you so.'"

I stifle a laugh. "Have you and Sean had dinner? I'm just leaving the office."

"Of course we did. It's after seven p.m. Would you like to come over for leftovers?"

"I'll be there in twenty minutes. Thanks, Alannah." I smirk as I end the call.

I made it to my sister's in less than twenty minutes since I got lucky and hit every green light. I pull up to her two-story colonial, lights shining through the windows of the first floor. I let myself in to find Alannah and Sean sitting on the couch watching reruns of *Will and Grace*.

"Do you two ever watch anything else?" I laugh, walking past them toward the kitchen, where Alannah has a plate of shepherd's pie waiting for me.

I grab a drink before taking my plate and a fork out to the living room to join them.

"Uncle, just because you wouldn't stand a chance with Debra Messing doesn't mean you have to disrespect a classic." Sean's response has me choking on my first bite of food.

Alannah is smiling at him with pride. We sit there for a few hours enjoying each other's presence watching the old sitcom.

"Can we at least all agree that Sean Hayes carried this series?" I look back and forth between the two of them for confirmation.

It's eleven p.m. before I get home, and I realize that Hadley hasn't called me. I send her a text to check on her.

Connor:

Mo ghrá, did you make it home safe?

I lie there for a few hours staring at the ceiling, worried that something is wrong since I haven't received a reply before sleep finally takes hold.

Chapter Twenty

K at, Ryan, and I meet at Finley's at five p.m., the table once again covered with all the favorites that we share. A few drinks down the hatch, and Kat and I grind on each other while Ryan sways back and forth near us. The jukebox is playing "Low" by Flo Rida, and Kat and I are living our best 2009 lives while Ryan watches us, laughing and shaking her head. I grab her wrist and get her sandwiched between us so we can dance together. She's stiff at first, but eventually loosens up so that we're all in sync with the music.

We get lost in the drinks that people keep buying us at the bar. The night passes so quickly that I lose track of time. At some point, it clicks to change to water so that I can drive. After my fourth glass of water, I tell the girls it's time to go, and we pile into my car so I can drop them off.

I'm finally pulling into the driveway at midnight. We shut down Finley's, which is a first for a weeknight. I put my car in park and pull out my phone to text Connor to see that I have no service.

What the hell?

I step out of my car, pressing the button on the remote to lock and arm it. I stride slowly toward the house, not in the mood to see Andy. When I reach the front door, I notice it's unlocked. Of course Andy would forget to lock the door.

Jackass.

I make it to my new bedroom and change into Connor's t-shirt, which is still on my bed. It doesn't smell like him anymore, and I give out a pouty huff. I really should trade it out for a fresh one. Still, I put it on and revel in the fact that it once touched his perfect physique. I climb into bed and curl up under the covers. Checking my phone one last time before I crash for the night, I notice I still have no signal. I send a goodnight text in case whatever the issue may be is resolved while I'm sleeping.

My phone alarm goes off only a few hours later. I pry my eyes open to find that six a.m. is already here. I groan as I sit up. Checking my phone, I see I still have no service. What the hell is going on?

I crawl out of bed and make my way to the hallway bathroom so I can shower before I get dressed for work.

Standing under the too-hot water, I lather my hair in my cinnamon and citrus scented shampoo, washing out the stench of the bar. After a moment, I rinse my hair to apply the conditioner. I let it sit for several minutes while I do a full body shave, guiding the razor up my legs, when I feel the shower door open. I stiffen, abruptly turning around to find Andy stark naked.

"What in the actual fuck do you think you are doing, Andy?" I scream when he tries to wrap his arms around me.

"Come on, Had. I've missed you." He tries to turn his charm on, but unfortunately for him, it's not working for me at the moment.

"No! Get out! If sleeping in a different room hasn't clued you in, I'm not interested in being close to you right now!"

"I don't give a rat's ass if you aren't interested. You're my *wife*, and you will do as you're told," he snarls.

"I'm fairly certain that doing what I was told is what got us to this place, so I'm going to pass," I sass back at him.

Without another word, I go to turn from Andy, hoping he gets the hint. That's when he grabs my wrist and spins me to face him. His arm winds back with an open palm, and he slaps me with a loud crack across the face. The harsh sting against my wet skin is so painful, my face jerks sharply to the side from the force.

I stand there in shock, not saying anything. His retreating form through the shower and then the bathroom doors is the last thing I see before I collapse onto the tile floor, tears stinging my eyes. I sit in silence, the scalding water prickling my skin as quiet sobs take over.

I make it to school only twenty minutes later than originally planned. A heavy layer of makeup covers the red mark. I'm not upset with how it turned out after watching a quick YouTube video on how to cover a red mark on the skin. Apparently, green concealer under my normal concealer does a hell of a job of covering the discoloration. Hopefully, I iced it long enough that the swelling doesn't become too noticeable throughout the day.

As I walk toward the entrance of the building, a text notification sounds. I pull out my phone to check before starting my day.

Connor:

Heya, mo ghrá, I'm glad you're OK. I was worried when I didn't hear from you last night. Meet me at the office after work. We can get dinner.

I smile at the screen. *This man is my everything.*

I gasp aloud at the realization. When did that happen? I can't be this far gone for him, can I?

Hadley:

I will let you know when I get out of here. The fifth shot of Jameson at Kat's insistence was the wrong move. I'm barely holding it together right now.

I feel guilty instantly. I'm not lying, yet an omission of the full truth is lying, isn't it?

Another message dings.

Connor:

Come over. I'll take care of you tonight, beautiful.

I don't respond; instead, I walk inside and get to the classroom I'll be in today. The kids aren't here yet, so I set my things down and sit behind the desk and get lost in my thoughts about this morning and the assault I endured.

Where did the monster in my shower come from and what happened to the man I married? He's never been like this before. Andy had never laid a finger on me in all the years we'd been together until now.

I'm torn from my thoughts when a commotion erupts as the kids pass through the classroom door and see me.

"Mrs. James, you're back!" one of the kids, a sweet blonde girl named Haley, squeals.

Chuckling at her excitement, I respond. "Of course I'm back. I told y'all I'd be popping in and out of your classes throughout the year when anyone needs a sub."

"Yay! We're so glad to have you back!" another one shouts from the back of the room.

The day goes on without a hitch. When the last bell rings, I walk into the bathroom and check my face. It's not as swollen as I expected, and that brings a smile, albeit a sore one, to my face. I pull my phone out of my pocket and respond to the text I've been avoiding all day.

Hadley:

Is the offer for dinner and a night with you still on the table?

The response is immediate, which makes me grin.

Connor:

You never have to ask. I would drop everything for you.

Chapter Twenty-One

Connor

"I expect to have at least three more contracts by the end of the month. The Quellin project is nearly done. They're going into the final phase of testing servers, which will be completed by the end of the week," I say to the owner of the company, who insisted on a conference call this afternoon.

"What are the projected numbers for the end of the year?" he asks.

"If we go through with Liam's proposal, we could anticipate at least fifteen more by the end of the year and would need to double the staff we have right now."

"Shit, Connor. What are you waiting for? Bring on Liam's company and let's do this. That will mean incredible things for the company," Mr. Dean replies.

"I'll send the message to move forward after we end this call." I smirk at my phone when I hear a tap on my door.

I look up to see Jordan peeking in. When I raise my brow in question, he moves aside, allowing Hadley to walk past him, closing the door behind her. My smirk turns into a full-on grin when I see her.

"Mr. Dean, I will take care of this now. If there is nothing else, I have some things to do." My response is clipped as I stand, walking toward Hadley and pulling her into my arms.

The bright smile that takes over her features when we reach each other is infectious. I hear Mr. Dean respond, but promptly ignore him and turn off the speakerphone.

"Mo ghrá," I say simply before pressing my lips to her.

When I take her face between my hands, I notice she stiffens briefly. I press my mouth against hers, flicking my tongue against her plump bottom lip, asking for more. Her lips part with a gasp that I take as an invitation and delve my tongue into her sweet warm mouth while we tangle ourselves together in a fervorous kiss. She moans into my mouth for just a second, sending shockwaves to my cock, which is already straining against the zipper of my slacks.

We pull apart panting.

"Oh, God. I've missed you, baby." She sighs into my chest.

"Beautiful, what is it?" I bring my hand to her chin, raising her face to meet my eyes.

"Just a rough day." She smiles weakly at me, looking away. "Let's go get dinner."

I don't push her, even though it's infuriating me that something is bothering her this much. I know that it's more than just a rough day. I can feel it in my bones. We walk out of the building hand-in-hand. Shockingly, we don't run into Mr. James.

Once we're finally at District Thai, just around the corner from my office, she visibly relaxes. She orders her favorites from the menu: bikini shrimp and pad kee mao. Meanwhile, I stick with their pineapple fried rice. I smile across the table at her. She looks lost in thought.

"Mo ghrá," I say gently, attempting to pull her out of her mind. "Talk to me, beautiful."

"It's nothing. My head still hurts is all." She returns my smile, but it doesn't touch her eyes like it should.

It takes little time for our food to be ready and delivered to the table. Like the last few times we've been here, I steal one of the shrimp appetizers. It's a shrimp wrapped in seaweed and a wonton, then deep-fried, and it is delicious.

I look up from my rice to find her nibbling on one of the crispy wonton-covered shrimps. I place my hand on her knee under the table, and she looks at me sweetly. Squeezing gently, I gaze into her eyes.

"Mo ghrá, how about I call it an early day and we go back to my place? We can cuddle up on the couch, and you can read."

Judging by the look on her face, you'd think I'd just offered her the moon, stars, and heavens all at once.

We've been lying on the couch together for an hour when I stand to go to the bathroom and relieve my bladder. When I walk back, I notice Hadley rubbing her cheek. As I stand back and watch her, I notice a faint bruise covering the side of her face. Seeing the discoloration, I feel my anger grow to a near boiling point in seconds.

I walk back to the couch and sit down. I instantly pull her toward me, caging her in my embrace. A soft giggle passes her lips as she relaxes into me.

"What's that for?" Her voice is lighter than it has been all night.

I pause for a moment.

"Mo ghrá, what happened to your face?" My question is barely a whisper.

She instantly stiffens, her hand cupping her cheek again.

"It's nothing. I'm fine." Her response is clipped.

"It's not fine. What happened? Who did this to you?" I growl.

She pulls away and turns toward me, tears pooling in the corners of her eyes. It's written all over her face. I feel heat erupt in my veins, the rise of anger blinding me, and all I can see is red. I shake my head just a bit, clearing the rage, and gently cup her cheek, pressing my lips to hers for only a brief moment. It takes every bit of strength I have not to storm out of here, find the motherfucker, and give him a few bruises myself. A growl vibrates from deep in my chest at the thought.

"Bodach! I will end him, mo ghrá," I grind out.

"No, baby. It's fine, really. I don't want him to darken our time together. I am okay. I promise." Her voice cracks.

"Stay with me. You can move in here. I'd love to have you here with me. Please, mo ghrá, stay with me?" I can hear the desperation in my voice.

"Oh, Connor," she breathes, pressing her forehead against mine. "I can't. He's still my husband. Even if he's an asshole."

"I won't accept this. You are mine. I don't care about any of the legalities involved. I will not allow him to harm you. Harm what's *mine*!" My volume grows until I roar out the last word.

She flinches at my response.

What the fuck does she expect me to do? Sit here and allow him to assault her? I don't care if they're married. She's mine. I will do whatever it takes to keep her safe.

I don't say anything for a while. I just bring her closer to me, wrapping myself around her and holding her. It takes every bit of restraint not to tie her to my bed and not let her leave when she stands up and tells me she needs to go home because of an early morning session with Kat.

"I need to be up at five. If I stay here, I'll have to be up earlier," she says softly.

"Let me know when you're home?"

It comes out as a question, but we both know if she doesn't, I'll show up at their house. As it is, I would like to bang down his door and tear him apart for what he's done to Hadley.

"Always, baby." She smiles shyly up at me through her dark lashes.

I stand to join her, my intention of walking her to her car clear. We walk silently, hand-in-hand, to her car. When we get there, I pause for a small moment, just taking her in. I quickly confine her to the side of the car, pinning her arms to her sides and pressing my hips against hers, keeping her in place. Lowering myself to her mouth, I run my tongue around the delicate lines of her lips. She gasps, instantly opening for me. I deepen the kiss, taking her in. Her sweet taste is still as intoxicating as the first time. After several minutes, with my cock is so fucking hard it's almost painful, I pull away.

"Please be safe. Call me if anything—and I mean *anything*—happens."

She smiles yet again, but nothing passes her lips this time.

Chapter Twenty-Two

I walk back into the foyer, my heart in my throat. His car isn't here, but that doesn't necessarily mean anything. I climb the stairs to my room and crash for the night. I have no desire to eat anything after the argument with Connor.

I can't believe I defended Andy's actions. What the hell is wrong with me? I know Connor is worried. Hell, if I'm honest, so am I. I didn't expect this to ever be my life.

I've been with Andy so long, though. The old him was never like this. I can get him back, can't I?

But do I even want to at this point?

The number of questions that spin through my mind is enough to make me dizzy. Locking my bedroom door, I change into Connor's shirt and lie down. Tears in my eyes, I grab my phone and send him a message.

Hadley:

I'm sorry, baby. I know you're concerned. It will be OK. I'll be fine.

Connor:

I swear to you, Hadley, if he lays a hand on you again, I'll fucking end him. The bodach.

I fall asleep with my phone in my hands, tears falling and staining my face again. I wake to a light tapping on my bedroom door. Checking my phone, I see it's only ten p.m.

"What do you want, Andy?" I groan from my spot on the bed.

"Can we talk, Had? Please?" His throat is scratchy, like he's been yelling all day. He sounds like a mess.

I climb out of bed and unlock the door. Andy peers down at me, eyes glistening with unshed tears. It doesn't look right, though. I don't know what it is; I can't quite put my finger on it. He drops to his knees, wrapping his arms around my waist. I stand there frozen, my arms in midair after jerking them up and out of his grasp. He talks into my shirt.

"Hadley, honey, I'm so sorry. It's just been so long since I've had you. I miss you so much. I lost my temper. Please, Had. Forgive me?"

I say nothing, unsure of what, if anything, I could say at this point.

"Had?" I can feel him move to look up at me.

I haven't moved, staring at the wall. I'm terrified. It feels like no time has passed, yet it seems that all the time in the world has passed us by.

I breathe out, "Andy, I don't know if I can forgive you. You're not the man I married anymore."

I feel his arms stiffen around my body. "I'm still the same man, honey. I am. I need one more chance, please. I'll do anything you want. We can close our marriage. Please. I only need you. I don't need Naomi or anyone else."

"Andy, I'm not losing Connor," I state as a matter of fact.

He stands up in a huff.

"Well, I'm not losing my fucking wife, Hadley. You are mine," he growls before he turns on his heels and stomps like a petulant child back to what was once our room.

I close my door and lock it again before returning to the bed, unease churning in my gut. I climb back under the covers and crash as soon as my head hits the pillow.

I wake to the alarm on my phone blaring some godawful tone I've never heard before. I silence it, seeing it's five a.m. I groan to myself, realizing I have a gym session with Kat. I stretch my limbs, warming them up before standing when I realize my door is wide open.

I gasp to myself. How the fuck did he manage to do that? These rooms don't have keys.

I sit up, turning off the alarm before I stand, then step out into the hall to go to the bathroom when I see Andy standing there, as if waiting for me. I gasp, clutching my chest.

"Andy, what are you doing?" I groan as I try to walk past him.

He moves directly in my path, not allowing me by.

"I told you, Had. You're mine. We *will* continue our conversation from last night." The coldness in his voice has me nervous.

"If you don't let me by, the only thing that's going to happen is I'm going to pee on the floor. God, is it too late to recast?" I ask, my annoyance clear.

With no warning, Andy grips a fistful of my hair. His free hand wraps around my throat as he glares into my eyes.

"I wouldn't be so smart-mouthed with me right now, *wife*." The way he says the word sends chills down my spine, and real fear courses through my body.

"Let me go," I gasp the words, trying to breathe through the pressure he's applying to my windpipe.

He says nothing, releasing my throat. I notice his fist cocked back only a half a second before it connects with my face. I hear something crunch as the blinding pain takes hold of me. I collapse onto the floor, my hands holding my face as the shock radiates through my body. It takes me a few moments to realize I have in fact peed myself.

I'm just aware enough of my surroundings that I hear Andy leave the house when the front door slams shut. Sobs wrack through my body, and tears and snot run down my face. I don't know what the hell happened here.

Where did we go wrong?

I sit for what could be hours before I remember I was supposed to meet with Kat. I send her a message so she doesn't worry.

I turn my phone off, not even waiting for a response. I crawl to my feet, standing on trembling legs, and make my way to the kitchen for ice and an aspirin. I grab the soft ice pack from the freezer and wrap it in a thin towel before placing it on my face. The coolness feels excruciating and satisfying, taking away some of the heat from my inflamed cheek.

The swelling is already starting; I can feel my face tightening from where he left his mark. The skin around my left eye is so taut, I can't open it to see anything. With my right eye open, I look down at my hands. I see they're covered in red, gooey liquid. Oh, God.

I run to the bathroom off the foyer and see blood dripping from the side of my face that took the impact. The tears and snot mixed with blood make my face look like I just bathed in someone's blood and resemble something out of a horror movie.

I've been staring at myself for the past twenty minutes in a daze when the front door opens. Immediately, I stiffen and shrink down against the wall to the floor next to the vanity, pulling my knees to my chest and making myself small on the floor in case it's him.

"Hadley? Are you here?" I hear Kat call.

Oh, my God. I can't face her. Not now. Not ever. Not like this.

I try to stay quiet, the soft whimpering sounds of my fear escaping without my consent. I hear her padding down the hall toward the bathroom where I'm hiding. I hear an abrupt gasp when she reaches the doorway, and I know I've been found. I glance up to see Kat's face, the color completely drained from her normally warm copper coloring with a horrified expression.

"Oh, babe, what happened?! Who did this to you?" She collapses on the ground next to me.

I shake my head, not ready to answer her. Saying nothing, she stands back up, grabs the dark hand towel hanging next to the sink, and runs it under the faucet to dampen it. She kneels in front of me, cleaning up the mess on my face so it doesn't dry any more than it already has, gently wiping away my blood.

Kat sits on the cool tile with me for hours, holding my hands before insisting we get up and walk out to the living room. We sit on the couch together, and I fall into her arms, sobbing into her chest. Her arms encase me in the safety I need, and I fall asleep wrapped in her embrace. Sometime later, unconsciousness fades, and I see that Ryan is now with us.

"Hey, bestie." She's so quiet, like she's worried she'll spook me if she speaks too loudly.

She's never spoken to me like this. It's as if she's afraid I'm going to break.

"Hi," I croak.

"Can you tell us what happened?" Ryan's softness is messing with me.

I shake my head at her, too ashamed of what's happening.

"Okay, you don't have to, but can you please stay with one of us until we can get to the bottom of this? We can't leave you here alone like this."

The door opens at that moment, and Andy rushes in. I stiffen in Kat's arms. She grips me tighter, and I know she knows, at the very least, who did this to me.

"Had, honey? What's going on?!" he shouts with faux concern, as if he doesn't know.

"Get the fuck out of here, you psychopath! What gives you the right?" It's Kat who responds, releasing me to stand, getting in his face and shouting at him.

"What the fuck, Kat?" Ryan and Andy ask simultaneously.

"You didn't just feel the way she tensed. This motherfucker is the one who did this to her," Kat snarls.

"What the fuck?" Ryan repeats, this time shooting an accusatory glare at Andy.

His hands shoot up in a defensive gesture.

"Kat, Ryan." I speak for the first time, my voice hoarse. "I am okay. Andy and I need to have a conversation."

"The hell you do. We're not leaving you," Ryan hisses.

"Please, I'm okay," I say with more confidence than I feel.

I don't know what it is, but I feel like I need to speak to Andy.

The glares that Ryan and Kat give me send chills down my spine.

"I swear to you. I'm fine. He will not hurt me," I say. "Will you, Andy?"

He nods his head in agreement.

"If he touches you again, I will never forgive you and I will kill him." Ryan levels me with a look of pure disgust.

She grabs Kat's hand and pulls her out behind her. Kat's protests become muffled once the front door is closed.

Andy and I stare at each other for what could be moments or hours, my head still spinning from the day's events. He strolls over to sit next to me like it's just another day. I shoot up from the spot I've been in since Kat brought me here this morning. I can't be this close to him; my body is physically revolting at the thought.

"Andy, I don't know what the hell has gotten into you. What has changed in the last five years to turn you into such a monster?"

I'm pacing back and forth in front of the couch. My filter is lacking, and I know it's dangerous for me to be so bold with him, especially alone right now, but I can't stop myself.

"I don't know. I thought I wanted to be with Naomi and with you. I thought I needed to experience more." His voice is shaking. "Hadley, I am so sorry. I don't know what's been coming over me. Please. Don't give up on me here. I will make it up to you, however you want. Please, baby girl."

I say nothing for a few moments, my stomach turning when he calls me "baby girl." This desperate begging, it's not a good look for him.

"You need to go to therapy." I break the silence. "Nothing about your actions is even remotely okay, you asshole. I will not be your punching bag." As I say the words, my heart breaks. "I don't want to lose Connor, and if he is willing to continue a friendship with me, I will stay friends with him. He means more to me than I can express to you. And you? You need to end things with Naomi."

Chapter Twenty-Three

Connor

I haven't been able to get a hold of Hadley for a few days. Her phone is going to voicemail. I've been trying to allow her space, but this has been painful. I have a terrible feeling rooted deep in my bones, my gut telling me that something isn't right. I grab my phone from my desk and scroll back to the group text I had with Ryan and Kat when they helped me with our date.

Connor:

> Howya, ladies. Have you heard from Hadley? Her phone has been going to voicemail for several days.

Kat:

> You should go check on her.

> Yeah, what Pickle said.

My heart drops to my stomach at their response. I snatch my keys from my desk before jumping to my feet and head to my car. Once inside, my mind is racing with how our conversation ended when I last saw her. My imagination is on overdrive, picturing all types of scenarios, none of them good.

I ignore every single light and stop sign, not giving a shite about any traffic laws until I am parked behind her car in the driveway, blocking her in. I push my door open harder than necessary, shutting it just as hard behind me, and race to the front door, halting when I am close enough to ring the bell. There's no answer for several moments, so I knock, hard. Internally, I know I must look like a psychopath out here, but I am so in love with this woman. I'm terrified of losing her.

I finally see movement through the closed curtains. The door cracks open and I see dark purple and yellow blotches through the hair she has curtaining her face. I push my way in as gently as I can to make sure I don't hurt her again.

"Mo ghrá," I gasp.

She says nothing, just stares at me with glassy eyes from the tears she's trying not to shed.

"Mo ghrá. What did he do to you, beautiful? Are you okay? Obviously not, but have you been to a doctor to make sure you don't have a concussion or any broken bones?" I pepper her with question after question.

Then her hair falls away from her face and I see the extent of how bad it is: her eye is nearly swollen shut, the entire side of her face is covered in a bruise, and there is a cut near her eyebrow.

"Is this why you haven't been answering my calls or texts?"

"Connor" she sobs, falling into my chest.

My name on her lips is usually one of my favorite sounds, but as she sobs, it breaks my heart.

"I...I started talking back and not taking his shit or manipulation, and he lost it the second time." She holds me tight. "I haven't been avoiding you. I turned my phone off the morning it happened after I canceled on Kat, and I haven't been able to find it. I would have asked Kat to get a hold of you, but she and Ryan aren't speaking to me right now. I'm so sorry." The words stream out in a shaky ramble.

"My love, you have nothing to fucking apologize for." My Irish brogue is coming out stronger than usual. "I will end the bodach." My words erupt in a snarl.

Hadley is still staring at me, taking me in like she did the first night we met. I realize something she said makes no sense.

"What do you mean, Kat and Ryan aren't speaking to you?"

"Because I made an agreement with Andy," she wheezes through new sobs.

My heart aches before she says the words, knowing what's coming next.

"I told him that if he went to therapy and ended things with Naomi, I'd try to work things out."

My heart shatters into pieces the moment she says the words.

"So, you're ending us?" My question is barely a whisper.

I haven't given my heart to anyone like this since I was in college. I vowed to never feel this pain again until Hadley.

"Baby, I'm so sorry. I don't want to lose you. I know I have no right to ask, but if there is any way we can maintain a friendship..." The words are rushed together and she can't even finish the thought.

She feels the same pain I do. Why is she doing this?

"Please don't call me that if you can't be with me," I say flatly. "I will be here. If you need anything, I'll be here. I will try a friendship, but my feelings for you go so much deeper than friendship. You know that." I peer into her eyes, knowing the mask holding in my emotions is faltering. "If you don't find your phone by tomorrow night, I'll have one delivered. If he touches you again, I don't care what time of day it is, you fucking call me. Don't you dare allow this to continue, Hadley. I will never fucking forgive myself for walking out this door if something happens to you. Do you understand me? If anything happens to you..." I swallow the sob trying to claw its way out of my chest. "I will never forgive myself, mo ghrá."

I know I shouldn't continue calling her that, but the term is as natural as breathing at this point. I press a kiss to her hair before I separate from her and walk out the door, leaving my heart broken at her feet.

I don't remember walking to my car or driving back to the office. I only come to when I get to Andy fucking James's floor. I see him hovering over Naomi's desk, whispering, and nearly lose my mind. I don't bother clearing the distance. I growl loudly across the open floor plan.

"Mr. James, my office, now!" My baritone cuts the chatter in the space to silence instantly.

I turn on my heels and stomp back to my office. I take the stairs, knowing that if I get stuck with him in the elevator, my fist will be through his face. When I get to my office, I see Jordan. The look on my face must say it all, because he turns a ghostly shade of white in an instant.

"Hold my calls. Do not interrupt this meeting for anything. Do you understand me?"

I don't bother waiting for him to respond. I walk past his desk and into my office. I barely have a moment to try to calm myself before Andy walks in.

"Close the fucking door," I snarl.

He does as I command without a word, and when he turns to face me, I see the tough exterior he's trying to display. It does nothing but piss me off even more. I close the distance between us, pushing him against the wall. My hand grips his throat hard.

His eyes go wide. That's good. At least I know he has the sense to be scared.

"I'll give you one guess as to who I just had the pleasure of seeing." I don't give him any chance to respond, not that he could since he's starting to turn red with the lack of oxygen. "I am telling you like I told her. If you ever fucking touch her again, you will not fucking walk this earth. How *dare* you beat your wife? She is perfect, and you had the balls to raise your hand to her not once, but twice. Hell, who knows if there's been more since before you insisted on opening your marriage so you could fuck your employee?"

I release him and walk away. He's gasping for breath.

"I never expected her to find someone else, let alone my boss. You fucking dick." His voice is hoarse.

"You're telling me because you felt the need to step outside of your marriage and forced her into saying yes to what *you* wanted, you still had the nerve to expect her to stay home and pine over you until you decided you were done with your extracurricular activities?" I spit the words, rage coursing through my body.

How can she choose this? Him? This can't be right.

"She's my wife, Connor. *Mine.* Not yours. She will never be yours." A wide grin spreads across his face. "Never. Again."

"I know all about your agreement. Don't think I won't tell her if I suspect you and Naomi are still fooling around. If you want to claim her, treat her like the fucking queen she is." I glare at him. "Get the fuck out of my office, and don't make me break her heart by not keeping your dick in your pants."

Nothing else needs to be said. Andy opens my door and walks out, leaving me alone. Jordan walks in several moments later.

"You need anything, boss?" His voice is laced with concern.

The poor kid must be scared shitless. I attempt to mask my mood and control my features before I respond.

"I'm good. I'm going to take the rest of the day off. Call my cell if you need anything." I stand, grabbing my laptop and briefcase before leaving my office.

I make it to my car before I pull my phone out and send a new text.

Connor:

> If you two don't hear from her before tomorrow morning, let me know.

I don't bother waiting for a response before I send another message.

Connor:

> I know you're both pissed at her. I am too, but do not leave her alone with this. That's not what she needs.

Kat:

> I'm so scared. He's going to kill her, and she won't let us do anything to get her out of there.

Ryan:

> I'm livid. She knows better than to do this.

She feels obligated. They're married, and as much as I fucking hate this and it's breaking my heart, I will put myself back together while doing everything in my power to keep her safe.

Chapter Twenty-Four

I've been searching for my phone for the last twenty-four hours with no luck. Andy got home at eleven last night, and when I asked him if he'd seen it, he glared at me and went to bed.

He hasn't really spoken to me since I told him the only way I'd try to make things work is if he ended things with Naomi. If his feelings are even remotely as strong as mine are for Connor, I can understand the difficulty, but I will not budge on this or my stipulation of therapy.

I go up the steps to his room and knock on the door.

"What, Hadley?" he grunts in greeting.

Oh, lovely.

"I've had no way of communicating with anyone for the past three days because I can't find my phone," I say softly, like I'm approaching a feral cat. "How was your day?"

"Apart from your boyfriend threatening me? It was fine." He pins me with a look that sends chills down my spine.

"I ended it with him today. I told you I would try." I pause. "How did Naomi take it?"

"So now you care about her feelings?" he growls.

"You have no one to blame here but yourself, Andy. Don't put this on me," I say flatly. "I told you I'd try if we closed the marriage and you went to a therapist to get help."

"I know what you fucking said," he snarls. "Go to bed, Hadley."

I don't bother responding, knowing it will just lead to more harsh words...or worse. My face can't handle any more of the latter.

I walk to my room, my phone still nowhere to be found. I crawl onto the bed and see Connor's shirt lying there. I don't even bother putting it on, instead just pulling it into my arms and holding it tight against my chest. As I lie down, my head falls onto the pillow and the tears flow freely down my swollen and sore cheeks. My heart aches so badly. I never wanted this.

I don't remember falling asleep, but when I wake, I'm still in the clothes I wore last night. I lie there for several moments reliving yesterday's events. The pain hits me all over again like a ton of bricks. The feelings I have for a man I've known for such a short period of time are making this pain unbearable. I hate being stuck here so much right now. Nothing is helping me relax, and I know If I leave the house, I will have to answer questions I'm just not prepared to answer.

Eventually, after I'm not even sure how long since I have no phone to tell the time and we have no clocks in the bedrooms—I would order one online if I had my damn phone—I climb out of bed and walk to the bathroom. After relieving my bladder, I check to see if Andy is home before I make the decision to shower. After the past few days, I don't trust him not to accept "no" as an answer.

Once I return to the bathroom, I turn the shower on and lock the door behind me. I peel yesterday's clothes off my body as the water warms. When it's finally at the point that Lucifer himself would feel comfortable, I step in and allow the scalding water to cascade down my body. My tears mix with the molten liquid as I allow the sobs to roll free while I know I'm alone.

I lather my hair in my citrus and cinnamon shampoo before rinsing, followed by my conditioner, and smooth it through all of my hair, covering each strand fully. I stand there under the water for a few moments while it works its way into the follicles before rinsing again, then take my time soaping up my body. The suds are so thick to remove the grimy feeling. When I've finally stood under the water long enough to no longer see any bubbles left on my body, I turn off the water.

I unlock and open the bathroom door once I've dressed and my hair is wrapped in a towel. The moment my foot hits the stairs, I hear banging on the front door. I slowly take the stairs one at a time, trying to peek out the windows by the front porch to see who is there. I hear the latch unlock, and I freeze only to see Kat and Ryan strolling in like they own the place.

"Jesus, you scared me," I say, my hand clutching my chest as the adrenaline flooding my body eases a little. "What are you doing here?"

"We were asked to drop this off," Ryan says as she hands me a new phone. "He's worried, just like we are."

Her pained expression is like a knife to the gut.

"I'm sorry. I wish I could explain it in a way that would make sense," I say quietly.

"You don't need to. He did," Kat chimes in this time.

I look at her with a question in my eyes.

"Connor," Ryan sighs, her exasperation clear. "Honestly, Hadley. We wish you'd met him first."

She says it like it's the most obvious thing in the world.

"You and me both," I say under my breath. "Thank you for this." I increase the octave of my voice a few decibels so they can hear me as I take the phone from Ryan's outstretched arm. "Do you want to stay for coffee?"

They look at each other briefly before turning back to me and nodding their heads.

We walk to the kitchen together, not saying anything as I brew a pot of coffee. We sit there in silence for several moments. Kat is the first one to speak, telling us about how she finally slept with Clay and he has the biggest penis she's ever had. Ryan and I chuckle at her lack of filter. Things slowly start to go back to normal and the conversation flows easily with every moment we're together.

I'm so glad they're here. I can't imagine life without them. If I'm honest, I also can't imagine life without Connor, and that scares me.

Even though he had them bring me a phone, I know I've broken him as badly as my face is broken, and it pains me greatly. We've finished four pots of coffee between the three of us and are ready to run a marathon when my new phone dings with a notification.

Mo Shíorghrá:

I'm here if you need me.

The name isn't what I had in my phone before, but I know it's him. I'm not sure what it means, but I know asking him to translate isn't the smartest choice for either of us. I simply respond.

Hadley:

Thank you. (heart emoji)

I exchange a look with the girls, and they both grab my hands to keep me steady from losing it even more than I already have at this entirely fucked-up situation.

Chapter Twenty-Five

Connor

Two weeks later

I've not been to the office since everything happened with Hadley. I don't trust myself not to pummel her bodach of a husband if I see him right now. She's texted me every day, and I've tried not to respond. It hurts so much. I've spoken to Ryan or Kat at least once a day since our initial text exchange so they can keep me apprised of how she's actually doing.

As much as I try to avoid the endearments, they slip out. I'm working from my sister's today, and let me tell you, Alannah is on the warpath. She's been itching to go to pay Hadley a visit, and as much as I love that my baby sister is ready to go defend my honor like this, it's not necessary. I may be broken—again—but I know Hadley never intended for this to happen.

"Brother," I hear Alannah call, pulling me from my thoughts.

I look up to see her standing directly across from me at her dining room table.

"How long have you been standing there?"

"Only a minute." Her gentle smile gives me some peace.

"What's going on?" I ask, putting my phone face-down on the table.

"I'm going to make breakfast. Do you want pancakes or waffles?"

"Yes, with home fries." I smirk at her.

"I've been kind for two weeks brother. Pick *one*." She pins me with an unamused look.

"Waffles." I pause. "And home fries?"

"Fine."

She laughs, and I join in. For the first time in two weeks, I laugh at something so silly. It's an unfamiliar feeling as of late.

Sean makes it to the table with us, just as breakfast is served. With a grumbled "Morning," he sits down and shoves his face full with two waffles and three heaping scoops of home fries.

Once he's fully awake, he gives me a weary look, and I raise a brow at him.

"What is it, boyo?"

"I asked someone out a couple of weeks ago, and I wanted to bring them home for dinner this weekend. I know you're going through it with

Hadley, so I understand if you don't want to be here, but I *really* want you to meet them."

Alannah stares at me, waiting for my response. She knew this was coming. Of course she did.

"Boyo, no matter what is going on in my life, I will always be here for you. You hear me, yeah?" I smile at him. "I would be honored to meet her."

His returning grin is all the response I need.

"Jordan, I understand. I will be back in the office tomorrow, and then back full-time next week. I have an important dinner tonight that I can't be late for, so I'm staying put for the rest of the day. Reschedule the meeting for tomorrow or one day next week."

"Okay, boss," he finally agrees.

Having been out of the office so long has apparently caused an issue with one of our new clients. They are insisting on an in-person meeting, and it's a major pain in my ass. I spend the next two hours finishing up the things that can't wait until tomorrow before finally closing my laptop to help Alannah finish up dinner.

By the time I get out to the kitchen, Alannah already has everything done that can be, so I set the table for us. Working quietly, I get lost in my thoughts until she breaks the silence.

"It's nice of you to do this for him even though you're hurting," she says gently.

"You know that boy means the world to me. I'd walk through fire for the kid," I reply simply.

And I would, no questions asked.

About twenty minutes after five p.m., Alannah's front door opens, and we hear Sean's voice and someone else whispering behind him. I see Sean first, tension rolling off him, followed by a tall kid with an athletic build quietly trailing behind. I share a smile with Alannah.

"Boyo!" I greet Sean as he walks in, wrapping him in a hug.

He squeezes me back, the tension easing from his body in my embrace. He pulls away and looks back at the boy he brought home for dinner.

"Mom, Uncle, this is my boyfriend, James." His wide grin, full of pride, spreads across his face.

"It's a pleasure, James. My name is Connor," I say, pulling him into a quick hug too.

The unease I saw on his face when he walked in behind Sean melts away just as quickly.

"I'm Alannah. It's so great to meet you, sweetheart," my sister sniffles.

I can't help but chuckle.

"Shut up, brother. It's sweet." She slaps my arm.

The four of us gather around Alannah's dining room table. I ask James a few questions to get to know him when Sean tosses a roll at my head. I catch it before it can make impact.

"Uncle, stop interrogating him."

I chuckle in response. "Okay, sis, you're up."

I wink at Alannah, who goes into a barrage of questions.

By the time we've finished dinner, we know everything we could hope to know about James, down to his first pet's name. Kirk, in case you were wondering. An orange asshole tabby. The kid's words, not ours.

I don't bother hiding my smile when James leaves. Sean looks between Alannah and I, his eyes glassy with unshed tears. Without a word, he crosses the distance between us and hugs us both. We stand there for several moments, the three of us holding on to each other. My sister's soft sniffles break my heart, knowing she's thinking about Sean's dad. When Sean pulls away, he looks up at me.

"Thank you for being here, Uncle."

"Boyo, there's nowhere I'd rather be tonight, but tell me, why are you sad?" I wrap an arm around his shoulders.

"I just wasn't sure. James isn't what you go for, and I just…"

I put my hand up, allowing the words to die on his lips.

"Boyo, I don't care if you date a man, a woman, or five men and women at once, so long as you are happy, responsible, and not hurting others." My serious gaze meets his unsure expression, which relaxes when he realizes my sincerity.

He doesn't say anything else, just stands there holding me close like he did when he was younger. I spend a few more hours with my little family before I say goodbye to Sean and Alannah, letting them know I'll be over for dinner later in the week before leaving for the night.

When I get to my car, I pull out my phone, noticing a missed text.

Andy:

I guess she isn't that important to you. Good to know.

Connor:

What are you talking about?

I spend a long while staring at my phone, waiting for a reply. When nothing comes, I dial Hadley's number. No answer, though it's after ten p.m., so she's likely sleeping.

I'll wait until tomorrow and try again. If my hair hadn't prematurely grayed, I'd blame her bodach of a husband for my silver locks.

Chapter Twenty-Six

Hadley

I enjoyed the day with my girls so much. I've needed it after everything that's happened with Andy. I'm still not sure how I feel about everything, and I'm hoping that he actually goes to therapy and works to get us back to where we were. We owe that to each other.

Ryan and Kat have made their opinion on giving him another chance very clear, but after all the time we've been together, the least I can do is try to save our marriage. If it can even be saved at all.

It's five p.m., the girls left about thirty minutes ago, and I'm debating what I want to do for dinner. Now that I have a phone, I consider getting takeout from the Chinese place that Andy and I used to order from fairly often. After perusing the menu, I text Andy to find out what he wants so I can place our order. Hopefully it will be here by the time he gets home.

Hadley:

Ordering from Asian Best. Do you want your usual or something different?

Andy:

How? You don't have your phone.

Hadley:

I got a new one. I was wanting to have dinner here when you got home. Do you know when you'll be back?

Andy:

The usual is fine. Be home in fifteen minutes.

Reading his last message, I find myself standing with my jaw hanging open. He's not been home this early in nearly a year. I dial the number for the restaurant and place my order quickly. I'm finishing picking up from my girls' day when Andy walks in with the bag of food in hand.

"How did you? What?" The confusion is apparent with my inability to complete one question before asking another.

"Huan pulled up as I was getting out of my car," he chuckles.

"Oh, makes sense," I reply as I cross the space between us and move to grab the bag from him so I can plate our dinner.

He grabs my wrist, and I tense. He pulls me to his chest with a softness in his eyes I haven't seen since before our anniversary dinner and presses a sweet, gentle kiss against my lips that has me looking up at him like a deer in the headlights. Unsure of what I should do or how to feel, I just stand there frozen, allowing him to press his lips to mine until I feel the attempts to deepen the kiss.

I push away from him abruptly.

"Andy, I'm not ready for that." My voice is barely a whisper; I'm terrified as to what his response is going to be.

He jerks back, and I flinch. The smirk that quirks at his lips has my stomach rolling.

"If you were this much of a prude with him, no wonder he's already with someone else." His snide tone takes me aback.

I know I have no right to expect Connor to wait for me when I can't promise him anything, but it hurts that he didn't tell me he started seeing someone else.

"I just want him to be happy," I say sincerely, my attempt at masking my features faltering as the weight of his words makes me admit something I've been fighting for weeks.

I am so irrevocably, deeply, madly in love with Connor. And I absolutely fucked it up.

I walk past Andy with the bag and work to get our dinner on plates, meeting him back in the dining room at our table. I sit quietly, taking small bites from the crab rangoon I ordered.

"Seriously, you're eating nothing but deep-fried cream cheese and wontons?" he asks, disgust clear in his tone.

I don't say anything, just sit there running through the last year or so in my mind. Now I realize he didn't start acting like this until about eight months ago. Nearly three months before he asked that we open our relationship.

"Andy, may I ask you something?" I look up at him through my dark lashes, not quite confident enough to meet his eyes.

"What?" The shortness strengthens my resolve.

I look him in the eye and open my mouth to ask the question when the doorbell rings. I stand to answer when he raises a brow as if to ask where I think I'm going when my face still looks like I went a few rounds in the ring. I lower myself back down, and he goes to answer the door.

I hear hushed voices and stand up, quietly strolling towards the opening of the corridor. I come to a halt as soon as I see Naomi at our front door...again. Her stomach is protruding just a little, and I realize what's happening before I step closer. The voices are clearer now.

"Naomi, I told you not to come here. I can't afford to lose her right now. The prenup my parents made us sign will give her everything if she finds out about us." I hear Andy's charm that used to be saved for me.

"I don't care, Andy. I'm not going through this alone. It's not just us anymore. We'll figure it out. Please, babe, we can deal with whatever we need to." I hear the tears in her voice.

My eyes prick with my own tears trying to break free. I don't want to admit it, but at the same time, I can't say I'm surprised. He's obviously still seeing her. Every word to me has been a lie.

I step into Naomi's view; her eyes go wide when she notices me, a sly smile on her face like she thinks she won some big prize. I can tell the moment she takes in my still-healing face, more yellow now from the incident so it doesn't look quite as bad as it had originally, her eyes rounding.

"What I gather from this..." I gesture between the two of them. "...is not only were you sleeping with her before you forced me into opening our marriage, but you haven't stopped seeing her after what you did to me and the agreement we made. You also got her pregnant?" I speak quickly, making sure I get it all out.

"Well, I guess congratulations are in order. Congratulations, Naomi. However, if you know what's best for you and that child, I would recommend not allowing him near either of you if he's going to do this..." I motion toward my face. "...to someone he's claimed to love for the past decade. You know, just some food for thought. If you'll excuse me."

I turn my back and make my way to the guest room where most of my clothes are, neither of them saying a word. I throw a duffel on the bed and toss in enough clothes for a few days so I can just get the hell out of here. I'll head over to Kat's and camp out for a few days while I figure out what I'm going to do.

When I have what I need in my bag, I toss the strap over my shoulder and turn to leave my room. Andy is in the doorway with a look of pure evil in his eyes that rivals Michael Myers. I walk toward him, my shoulders pushed back with all the confidence I can muster. As I try to pass him, I'm shoved backward toward the dresser, the corner jabbing my kidney. The pained gasp that escapes my lips is a sound I've never heard before.

His hand wraps around my throat, squeezing so tight that breathing is nearly impossible. My hands instinctively reach for his in an attempt to free myself from his grip. He's still pressing me so hard against the dresser, the wooden corner stabbing into my back. Tears roll down my cheeks as I struggle to breathe.

"Andy," I rasp. "Please."

I'm losing this battle. I ball my hands into fists, hitting him, trying to fight my way free.

"You're..."

I can only get one word out at a time.

"Going..." I wheeze, trying to get some air back into my lungs. "To..."

My eyes go wide as the darkness starts to cloud my vision.

"Kill..."

Everything turns to black before I can finish the sentence.

I don't know how long it's been since Andy choked me into unconsciousness. My eyes flicker open to a room covered in shadows, a mixture of moonlight and streetlamps shining through the window. I'm curled on my side on the floor of my room. I gasp, clutching my throat, sobs of relief wracking through me when I realize I'm alive.

That is, until I hear his dark chuckle.

"I couldn't let you go that easily. Not after you've ruined everything for me." His icy tone shoots terror down my spine.

"Andy, please just let me walk away," I beg as I struggle to my knees. "I won't tell anyone. Just please let me go."

I sure as hell *will* tell someone...as soon as I'm far away from the psychopath in front of me. As much as I try to mask my emotions, my adrenaline is too high right now to make it believable, and I know he sees right through the lie.

"Nice try, Had." He sneers.

He stands up and crosses the room from where he sat on the bed. His hand grips the back of my head, yanking my hair tight so I'm looking up at him.

"If only you could have kept your fucking mouth shut and left well enough alone. You could have spent the last year that our prenup requires in peace by yourself while I was with Naomi and our child. But no, you had to go and ruin everything." He shoves me down to the floor again.

Before I can take another breath, a blunt force steals the air from my lungs. I realize he's kicking me in my stomach and ribs.

It lasts for minutes? Hours? Days? I'm not sure.

When his leg gets tired, he pulls me back up by my hair. While he pants through his exhaustion, I look up at him, defiance in my eyes—a mistake I realize a second too late, as I see his closed fist is en route to connect with my already-broken face.

Chapter Twenty-Seven

Connor

I step into my office for the first time in nearly a week. I still haven't heard from Hadley, and quite frankly, I'm starting to worry. At this point, I came to the office to see if I can get anything from Andy. I know, how pathetic.

I'm the first one here, so I take a seat at my desk and pull the laptop from my bag. After spending the first hour in the office with uninterrupted time checking and responding to email, I hear a knock on my door. Looking up, I see Jordan. I motion for him to come in and shut the door.

"Hey, boss. Is everything okay?" he asks.

"It will be." I smile at him. "How has it been here, apart from pissing off Ms. Phillips? I knew I shouldn't have kept putting her off. She's going to cause a nightmare for us, isn't she?"

I rake my hand through my hair in frustration.

"It's been fine," he chuckles, ignoring my second rhetorical question. "You have a meeting later today with Mr. James, at his request."

"Why?" I raise a brow at him.

Jordan knows that I was seeing Hadley. Hell, he was just outside the door when everything went down in my office only a few weeks ago.

"He didn't say. Just said it was important. He sent me a text about twenty minutes ago." He shrugs, as if it shouldn't be a big deal.

"Alright. Well, let me know when Ms. Phillips gets here. I'm going to make the rounds. I'll have my phone on me."

I'm on the second floor of the building speaking with Gina Avery, part of the legal counsel that we have based out of our office to ensure contracts are addressed as swiftly as possible. We're chatting about several concerns that have been raised regarding verbiage for the Pacent Industries project that she believes Ms. Philips is causing a commotion about. The contract reads that they will owe us over five million for a six-month period. I nearly choke when Gina tells me about the typo in the contract.

"Christ, no wonder she's throwing a fit." I roll my eyes. "Hopefully this will be a quick meeting, then. Can you have the updated documents on my desk in the next thirty minutes?"

"Jordan already has it." She mockingly dusts off her shoulder as she smirks, spinning to walk back to her office.

I move through each floor, getting some face time with as many of my employees as I can. I like to try doing this at least once a day when possible. I enjoy catching up with everyone. They deal with situations for the company just like I do, and I appreciate their dedication. Unless I'm going to show my face and express that frequently, it will come off as insincere. I want them to know their hard work means something more than just a quarterly email.

I'm walking back toward the elevator when I get a message from Jordan indicating that Ms. Phillips is waiting in my office. With a heavy sigh, I step onto the elevator and press the button to go up.

Let's get this over with.

"Ms. Phillips," I say, extending my hand in greeting.

She takes it in hers, shaking it gingerly.

"I do apologize for having to reschedule so last minute yesterday. I had an important family situation come up. I appreciate your patience in agreeing to see me today."

I see the twinkle in her eye that she tends to get when I speak to her.

"Oh, Connor. Will you ever call me Lisa?" She places her free hand on my bicep in an obvious attempt at flirting, and the only way my dick could be any softer would be if Elsa were to show up and put the building in an everlasting winter.

"I prefer to keep things professional, Ms. Phillips," I respond dryly, stepping away from her overzealous hand. "Please, follow me."

I stroll into my office and take my seat behind my desk.

"Okay, Connor." She winks at me. "On a professional note, how the hell do you think you can bend me over, trying to get Pacent Industries to fork over five million dollars for a six-month contract?"

I blanch at her continuous flirting. "I apologize for the inconvenience this has caused. It's unfortunate, but it appears that there was a section missing and incorrect pricing in the contract we sent over. I have the correct information here."

I hand her the new contract indicating three million for a six-month contract or five million for a one-year contract. Her eyes skim over the updated pieces, and she licks her fingertips before flipping each page. I can see her gaze flicker to me each time she does it. She thinks she's being seductive, when in reality I'd rather gouge my eyes out.

"This looks sufficient. Do you have a pen, Connor?" she asks sweetly.

I hand her a pen, and her fingers purposely brush mine while my eyes nearly roll out of the back of my head when she looks down to the paper to sign. When she completes the multiple signatures required, she leans across the desk and slides the contract back to me, her chest nearly popping out of her shirt that I swear wasn't that revealing when she first sat down. I jerk my hand back when I realize what she's doing. I don't even bother trying to mask the disgust on my face.

"Ms. Phillips, this is highly unprofessional and inappropriate. If you cannot respect the boundaries I have been attempting to put in place here, I will have no choice but to tear up this contract before we even start, and I will be informing Mr. Pacent of the reason why we will not be going into business with Pacent Industries," I say coldly.

"Connor..."

She stares at me for a moment, reconsidering.

"Mr. Quinn," she starts again. "I am so sorry. Please. I thought you were playing hard to get. I will maintain a professional boundary from here on out."

I nod once at her and motion for her to leave.

"Jordan, in here, now!" I shout as soon as Ms. Phillips leaves.

"Yea, boss?" An apprehensive look crosses his face.

"Any future meetings with Ms. Phillips need to be conducted in the conference room with her project manager and the team," I snap.

It's not his fault. I'm just still so thrown at how much she tried to push the issue.

"I'm not mad at you. She just pushed it too far," I explain in a reassuring tone.

"Will do, boss." He nods before walking back out.

I'm sitting with my head in my hands for a few moments before I grab my phone to try Hadley again. I find her contact and press the green call button. The line rings several times before I hear a soft knock on my office door. I hang up and put my phone down.

"Come in," I say loud enough for anyone on the other side to hear.

The door opens to reveal Andy standing there with a smug grin on his face.

"Ah, Connor! Just the man I was looking for."

"How may I help you, Andy?" I raise a brow at him, schooling my face into a look of indifference.

"I'm just amused that you claimed you were so into my wife, yet you had some special dinner last night." He snorts.

"Yes, I did have a special dinner last night. With my family. How do you even know about that?" I try to keep my tone flat, worry sitting in my gut like a rock about where he's trying to go with this.

"I came up to speak with you about our *situation* yesterday when I heard that Jordan had just spoken to you about it and that's why you were refusing to show your face," he taunts triumphantly.

"Not that it is any of your business, but I had an important situation I needed to be there for with my sister and nephew." I glare at him, rage simmering just below the surface.

"Sure." He rolls his eyes. "Just stop contacting my wife. She told you we're together now."

The evil smirk that pulls at his lips leaves me uneasy.

"That is Hadley's choice to make. She's an adult, and if she doesn't want my friendship, she can tell me herself."

My resolve to go to their house to check on her after he leaves my office solidifies. Something isn't right.

"No, it's *my* choice." He winks.

I see a gleam in his eye as something clicks inside him. I barely have a moment to register before I see the semi-automatic pistol he's raising to my eye level.

"Andy, this isn't necessary." I try to keep my voice calm, though my thoughts are immediately with Hadley.

Jesus, what has this asshole done?

"What isn't necessary is you fucking my wife, Connor. I don't give a shit who you are. Just because I'm fucking someone else doesn't mean I actually expected *her* to go out and slip into someone else's bed. The bitch is MINE!" he barks at me.

"If you're going to shoot me for being with Hadley, then do it, because I wouldn't change a damn thing. She means the world to me, but you will *not* talk about her that way."

He sounds like a hyena when he responds. "Let's see if you really feel like you have a leg to stand on after this."

He lowers the gun, aiming toward my leg, when I see a blur coming at us. I flinch and drop low as a shot sounds from the gun, and I hear a body hit the ground near me in the next moment. Andy is cursing at someone to get off of him. Rising to my feet, I notice that Liam Asher has him pinned down.

"I'd ask what the hell you're doing here, but I could kiss you for your timing."

I nod to Liam in thanks as I grab my phone from my desk and dial 911.

Chapter Twenty-Eight

Hot, wet tears roll down my cheeks as I step into my bathroom, wearing a ratty old band t-shirt and sleep shorts. Didn't want to ruin any of my nice clothes.

Maybe the girls can donate them.

I step into the tub and sit down.

Connor has moved on. Andy tried to kill me. Kat and Ryan were right.

A sob wracks through my chest. I'm just...done. I can't do this anymore. I can't be this person. I'm done.

Unable to catch my breath, I send the text I prepared to my group chat, then turn my phone off. Avenged Sevenfold's "I Won't See You Tonight" blares on repeat through my Bluetooth speaker. I take the razor in my hand and, with trembling fingers, press the blade into the delicate skin of my wrist, cutting several inches down my forearm before repeating the process on the other side.

The pain feels good, relieving the inner turmoil I've been dealing with for weeks. Blood pools around me as I lie on the white porcelain. Silence slowly engulfs me, the music fading to a quiet hum before the darkness pulls me under.

Finally, I'll have peace. He can't keep me locked away. Can't hurt me anymore.

Through the darkness, there's a flurry of voices surrounding me.

No, I want the quiet back.

They keep calling my name, yelling at me to come back.

No, I don't want to. I will not be his doormat anymore. I will not go through this pain every day. Not anymore.

"Hadley, baby, wake up! Come back to us!"

I recognize that voice. Kat? She's supposed to be at work. Why is she here?

"God damn it, Hadley, don't fucking do this." This time, it's Ryan's sobs that filter through the haze.

Oh, God. What have I done?

I barely recognize the bright fluorescent lights flickering into view as they race by above me. How am I moving so quickly when my legs are still? Why is it so loud here?

"We're going to need A positive NOW!" I hear someone yell in the distance.

The darkness takes hold of me before another thought can cross my mind.

"Hadley Veronica James, I swear to God. If you don't wake up, I will never forgive you." Ryan's voice cuts through the fog.

"Ryan, shut up. Let her wake up before you yell at her," Kat whispers.

"Fuck that. I can't yell at her when she wakes up, Pickle," Ryan groans.

I feel someone grab my hand and squeeze.

"Come back to us, baby. We'll kill each other without you." It's barely a whisper, but I hear the pain in Kat's voice.

I feel her lean down close to my ear before she starts singing in a quiet murmur just barely loud enough for me to hear.

A tearful Kat sings a jumbled version of Hakuna matata. She pauses briefly, her voice shakes as she says, "Or something like that. Hakuna matata. Come back to us, baby."

There's a soft hum emanating throughout the room, and I hear a clicking sound before I lose myself to the haze of darkness once more.

My eyes flutter open. I know I'm in a hospital, but how long have I been here? Why can't I feel my legs?

I jerk up, but I don't make it far.

Why can't I move? I look down at my wrists—one, then the other. I'm bound to the bed.

I scream out in a panic. "Help! Help! What have you done to my legs?"

As the last words leave my lips, Kat and Ryan bolt upright from on top of my legs, and I realize they were holding me down.

With a sigh of relief, I relax back into the bed when a nurse dressed in plum-colored scrubs comes running in. She's an older woman with graying hair. It's not quite the beautiful silver of Connor's, though.

I flinch; just the thought of him shatters my already-broken heart.

"You're alright. Breathe," Nurse Plum says, trying to soothe me. "Okay, sweetheart, I'm Nurse Lily. Can you tell me your full name?"

Kat and Ryan are still quiet, just staring at me with tears in their eyes.

"Hadley Lancaster... James." I nearly gag as I say my last name.

Fear stirs in my gut at the thought of Andy. I need to file for divorce before I leave this room. Can I do that?

"Great, sweetheart. Do you know what day it is?" Nurse Plum continues her line of questioning.

"Considering I don't know how long I've been asleep, I'm gonna skip that question." I glare at her.

I see her lips twitch, fighting a smirk at my sass.

"Okay, last one. Do you know why you're in the hospital?"

I look at Kat and Ryan, gripping each other's hands like they're afraid I'm going to disappear in front of them.

"I slit my wrists because it was the only way I saw out of the situation with my husband," I whisper as my tears fall down my cheeks. "I'm so sorry, you guys. I should have listened when you tried to get me out. I was so ashamed that it had gotten as bad as it did. I always said I'd never be that girl. I'm so sorry I put you through that. I'm so sorry I scared you and hurt you. I'm just so sorry."

My shoulders are shaking violently as the sobs wrack through my body. Shame blankets me, and I can't even look at my two best friends. I feel the bed shift on either side of me and Kat and Ryan's arms holding me in a tight embrace, their sobs joining mine.

Before Nurse Plum leaves, she explains that not only did I have excessive blood loss, but I had severe internal bleeding, broken ribs, wrists and a concussion from the multiple beatings I had the *pleasure* of experiencing at Andy's hands. I had to have emergency surgery to stop the hemorrhaging. They had me sedated for several days in an attempt to help me rest comfortably.

If they only knew the emotional turmoil I've been in waiting to talk to my people.

As I sit in day four of inpatient therapy, the therapist assigned to my case, Amy, is going on about how Andy is a dick for manipulating and gaslighting me. Her short, blonde pixie cut suits her feisty attitude. I didn't think a therapist would be so frank with their opinions. I like her.

"It sounds like you aren't mad that he wanted to open the relationship anymore, though." She raises her brow.

"Honestly, no. Meeting Connor felt so right. I was mad at Andy in the beginning. I couldn't understand why he would want to open our marriage. Looking back, I realize he was already sleeping with Naomi and just wanted to be able to take her out without risking it getting back to me. You know, the entire having your cake and eating it too?" I scoff. "The more I think about it, I know Connor is my moose. I just need to get better before I can reach out to him again and try to fix this. If there's even a chance he'll take me back."

"Your moose?" She giggles and looks like she's lost in a memory; a warm smile brightens her face. "That will never get old."

I raise a brow at her and shake my head. "I need to get into a solid space with myself. I need a place to live. I know either Kat or Ryan will let me crash with them for as long as I need to when I get out of here, but I need to find my independence. I was with Andy for so long. I lived for him for nearly half of my life. I need to live for myself now."

My heart aches with pride in my declaration. Even if I never get another chance with Connor, I know I'll be okay. I'll have my girls by my side, and I'll have *me*.

"Well, for what it's worth..." She smiles at me. "I think you're going to be okay. We're going to have to keep seeing each other for a while, but I'm confident that so long as we make sure you are staying a safe distance from Andy, you will be okay to go home tomorrow. However, you will have my cellphone number should you have any triggers. You call me at any time if you can't find help."

"Really?" My smile nearly splits my face in two.

"Yes. Now go call Kat and Ryan and make sure they can pick you up. Our session is over today. We'll have another before you leave in the morning."

Amy's gentle smile warms my heart. She's a badass, but she has a genuine love for her clients that makes me feel like I'm not just a number, which I always thought with therapists. She's good people.

Chapter Twenty-Nine

I've been bouncing back and forth between Kat's and Ryan's for the last two weeks. Really, it's been the three of us going back and forth between the two of their places. I found an apartment today, though, so it will be back to us all staying on our own soon enough. Tonight, we're at Kat's, and as soon as Ryan and I walk in, we see that she's decided to torment us with a charcuterie board of all things pickle. Ryan and I exchange a look that says *we're ordering takeout.*

"I have something to tell you both." I take a deep breath before continuing.

I see two sets of eyes boring into my soul.

"I found an apartment this afternoon."

"Oh, my God!" Ryan screams.

"Oh, baby, I'm so happy for you!" Kat squeals. "You know we'd love to have you with us forever, but this is so important in your healing process."

"I may need you guys to stay with me for a night or two when I get settled, but I'm really excited to do this on my own." I smile halfheartedly.

"Babe, do you think you're ready to talk to him?" Ryan asks as she pulls my hand into hers.

I just shake my head. I have no idea what to say to Connor right now. How am I supposed to explain to him that I disappeared from the face of the earth because I tried to kill myself?

When I woke in the hospital, the phone he had sent me was missing, and I was so far gone in my own fear and depression that they had to lock me up for a week before I was deemed safe to rejoin society. I know he's been texting the girls, but I've asked that they not relay any of the specifics to him. The thought of him knowing...

I feel so ashamed. It's something that Amy is working on with me, understanding that feeling shame is normal, but also understanding that the situation was not my fault.

I haven't heard from Andy since the day he left me unconscious on the lush cream carpet of my bedroom. The police came to the hospital, saying that they had arrested him for assault and he was currently in jail.

I didn't ask any questions. I was just so damn thankful he wasn't going to be able to get to me again.

It's the first time I've come back to my house since that day. Kat and Ryan came with me so I could grab my things, but my demons from that night keep whispering in my ear. Knowing I'm not strong or stable enough to go through these doors on my own, I asked Amy to join the three of us. Kat and Ryan will do anything for me, but Amy can talk me off a cliff I didn't even know I was on before I jumped. I need my full support system.

I take the lead to the front door before stopping and staring up at it, the red door mocking me. I was in a puddle of my own blood as red as the paint that covers this door the last time I was here. I nearly lost my life behind these walls. I take a deep, steadying breath and turn the knob, pushing open the wounds that have just barely begun to heal.

I take a step through the threshold, and my breath comes in shaky gasps as I grip my two best friends' hands. I manage to make it up to the second floor, where the worst of the attacks happened.

I step into my room and see my once-beautiful cream carpet speckled in dark red dried blood. My stomach heaves when I see it, and I turn back, running into the bathroom and vomiting in the sink. Amy is behind me, holding my hair in a low ponytail to keep it from becoming an innocent bystander of the ejection my stomach is enforcing.

When I'm finally well enough to stand, I realize where I am and look at the tub. The pearl-white porcelain basin is now stained with a pink tint from my suicide attempt. I stare at the empty tub, thinking back on the last three weeks.

My two best friends never left my side, not once. I always had at least one of them with me. They'd only leave long enough to shower and then tag the other out. When my mom found out, she yelled at me and told me I was selfish for what I did. We haven't spoken since her outburst at me. After so many sessions with Amy, I know that my actions weren't selfish. They were actions of desperation and a need to escape a situation I was afraid to ask for help to get out of.

I wish I could say the only person to blame here is Andy, but I know I could have crawled out of the house to get help instead of into this room. What matters, though, is that I've forgiven myself.

I look back at Amy and take a deep breath. "Why is it easier to see this than it was to see the other room?"

"What happened to you in this room was a decision you made. What happened out there…" She points over her shoulder toward my room, where the carpet is stained with my blood. "That is something that happened *to* you. You've made amazing progress, but it's going to take time. Give yourself grace."

Amy and I stand in the bathroom in silence for a few more moments before we step back into the hall. I came here to do what I needed to. I don't need to bring any of the past with me. The four of us leave, and I feel like a weight has been lifted.

We finally get everything situated around my new home, which isn't a lot. I splurged on a bed, a couch, and some things for the kitchen. The pizza we ordered sits half-eaten on a makeshift coffee table made from a large plastic tub. Ryan, Kat, and I sit on my new couch, scrolling through online articles and ratings for local divorce lawyers. I may not have been able to file for divorce while I was still in the hospital, but it's absolutely happening as soon as possible.

I'm ready to take back my life in every way.

Chapter Thirty

Connor

"How are you doing?" Liam says through the speaker.

I hear his kids chattering in the background. He's become a good friend since the attack. I owe him my life, a debt I can never repay.

"I'm alright. I'm keeping busy," I respond, like he doesn't know I'm going out of my mind.

I know something happened to Hadley. I heard the police say that Andy was wanted for aggravated assault and attempted murder when they were cuffing him.

"Keep trying. Kay and I saw the way you both looked at each other. Don't give that up." I can hear the smile in his voice.

Sometimes the love he shares with his wife is sickening. Granted, right now I'm incredibly jealous because I miss my woman, so that may be clouding my opinion. We chat for a few more minutes about work until I hear Kayleigh call him for dinner.

Picking up my phone, I send yet another text.

Connor:

Can you please tell me something? Anything? It's been a month.

Kat:

You know we can't. It's her story to tell. I will say she's doing better. We're trying, Connor.

Ryan doesn't chime in, meaning they're probably with her. I'm glad. I asked them to stick by her side, and they have. Completely.

I've been staying with my sister and Sean since the incident. Alannah has dealt with so much shite that no one should have to face. Adding in what happened at my office has only made it worse. Sean has become my shadow, only straying when I force him to go to school. It's like it was right after his dad passed away, the two of them clinging to me like a life raft.

We're sitting on their couch, Sean leaning into my side and Alannah staring at the two of us while we watch *Will and Grace* yet again. Jack just burst into Will's office and they are singing a show tune when suddenly Jack is up and dancing ballet in front of Will's desk. Something clicks into place in my mind. I look from Alannah to Sean and back.

"Did you name him after Sean Hayes?" I raise a brow at my sister.

"You're just now catching on to that, brother?" She's laughing at me.

"Apparently I'm slow on the uptake," I chuckle.

It's just after midnight when we head our separate ways for the night. I climb into the spare bed I've been calling mine for the last month and stare at the ceiling.

It's like this every night lately. I grab my phone and open up my music app, hitting the playlist I've had on repeat since I haven't been able to see her. I fall asleep to memories of her beautiful face and the cinnamon and citrus scent that I'll never get enough of.

I jolt awake, a light sheen of sweat covering my skin. The dreams I've been having are so realistic. It's always the same: Andy attacks Hadley and I'm frozen in place, unable to stop it. Then we're back in my office and he takes me out before I can tell her how I feel.

I scrub my hands against my face in an attempt to get the images out of my mind. I look at the clock and it's five-thirty a.m. I still have thirty minutes before I need to get up for work; however, my inability to sleep through to my alarm has found me at Mud House more often than not. Today, it seems, will be no different.

I throw off my blanket and roll out of bed. In a sleep-filled haze, I take a quick shower and get dressed for the day. My black Armani suit fits like a glove, and the ivy-green button-up underneath my jacket complements my Irish complexion. I walk to the kitchen to see if anyone else is awake, but both Alannah and Sean are still in bed, so I leave a note on the kitchen counter that I'm headed out early.

The drive to Mud House is short, and I pull up to see Kayleigh getting out of her Subaru. Her bright smile instantly warms my heart. She's waiting for me when I step out of the car.

"You are here obnoxiously early, Connor." She laughs.

"Yeah, I haven't been sleeping well and I could use a very large cup of your cafe americano." I smile at her.

"Come on." She waves her hand, gesturing for me to follow. She pauses for a moment, giving me a gentle look. "Liam told me you still haven't heard from her. Give her some time. I know he's told you what we went through, but everyone handles their traumas differently. She'll come around. You're her moose." She winks at me.

I follow Kayleigh into Mud House, chuckling to myself. The stories she and Liam have told me about early on in their relationship give me some hope for my future with Hadley. They've built a beautiful life together, and their kids are cute little hysterical monsters.

I lean against the counter chatting with Kayleigh while she gets machines turned on and starts my drink.

Her best friend, Jana, steps out from the back and grins at me. "Hey there, Mr. Fantastic."

I don't really understand the reference, but it's a thing she does, so I've been told to just go with it.

"Good morning, Jana."

The three of us chat for a while, and when I notice it's close enough to six-thirty a.m., I bid them farewell and head to the office.

I step onto the elevator to head upstairs when I see Naomi coming in behind me. I hold the door for her so she can ride up with me. She has dark circles under her eyes, and she looks thoroughly exhausted. The project manager that took over for Andy has told me she's been having a rough pregnancy with lots of pain and morning sickness.

"How are you doing with everything?" I ask, not bothering with pleasantries.

Andy had made comments that she knew what he did to Hadley and didn't do anything about it. I have a hard time having much sympathy for her.

"I don't know. I didn't think it would go as far as it did." She looks up at me through dark lashes. "I didn't know how bad it was. He told me he slapped her…" Her voice cracks. "But I didn't know how bad it was until I saw her the night before he came after you. I should have told someone."

I grunt in response. What else can I say?

The elevator dings at her floor, the doors open, and she walks out without another word.

My day drags by at a snail's pace. I'm stuck in a meeting with Gina, the head of my legal team, until after five o'clock to discuss more contracts when I finally tell her I need to leave. My head is just not in it today. The lack of sleep has been getting to me so much more toward the end of each workday.

I head down to my car, leaving my laptop and everything at the office for the first time since I started here years ago.

When I finally get to my car, my body is on autopilot. Before I realize it, I'm getting out at Mud House. Apparently my body decided it needs a jolt. Stepping inside, I see Liam and Kayleigh talking at the counter. He turns toward me and smiles, walking over and wrapping his arms around my shoulders.

"How're you doing, Con?" His genuine concern is still something I'm not quite used to.

"I'm trying to get past that three p.m. crash." I say simply as I walk to the counter, not wanting to put words to the way I really feel.

Kayleigh already has my drink ready. I go to pull out my wallet to pay when my phone dings with a notification that has me frozen in place.

Chapter Thirty-One

I'm sitting in front of a classroom full of students. We've just returned from winter break, and everyone is complaining that we haven't had a snow day yet. It's been so unseasonably warm for this time of year; I have a tank top underneath my zip-up hoodie, and it's almost uncomfortable.

All I can think while they're complaining is, *I want to be snowed in with Connor.*

It's been six weeks since the attack and I'm *finally* feeling like myself again. The confidence I have in who I am and what I want is unlike anything I've ever felt before.

Once the lunch bell rings, I dismiss the kids to go to the cafeteria while I go back and sit behind my desk. I pull my phone out of my desk drawer and send a text to a number I've held close to me since she gave it to me. No one knows we've been in communication. I couldn't bear to not know how he was doing, and I knew she wouldn't sugarcoat anything. I need her brand of candidness.

Hadley:

> Do you think you could come over tonight? I'm ready, but I would like to speak to you first.

Her response is timely, as always.

Alannah:

> Don't mess with him, Hadley. I don't care how much he cares about you. I will not allow you to hurt him again.

Hadley:

> You know it was never my intention. There is so much more than what I've been able to tell you. Please come by tonight, and I'll explain what I can. Some things, though, I need to tell him first.

Alannah:

> I'll be there at five. Have a red wine ready and breathing when I get there.

I smile at her response. I love that she is so protective of Connor. It's made the time apart so much more bearable, knowing that she's looking out for him. As much as I want to tell the girls I'm ready, I know the instant they see the words, they'll tell him, and I can't have that. I need to be the one to reach out first.

The lunch period goes by quickly. I'm with second-graders today, so I still have thirty minutes to eat the PB&J sandwich I brought from home. I've been eating like one of my students for the last week, and I know it's because my nerves are shot.

I just hope I didn't take too long. The thought of losing him permanently... I can't imagine a life without Connor in it.

I pull up to the parking lot of my apartment building and see Alannah leaning against her car, a look of frustration plastered on her face. I park my car and get out, grabbing the bottle of wine she asked for. I hand it over, a peace offering.

"Hey," I nearly whisper.

God, this is going to be even worse when I see him.

"Let's get this over with, Hadley." Her response is clipped.

I lead the way to my door. She follows me inside and takes a seat on the couch, her posture tense. I grab two plastic cups from my kitchen and pour us each a healthy serving. Handing her one, I keep the other for myself and sit facing her on the couch. I tuck my leg under myself and take a generous sip before I look at her. Taking a deep breath in, I tell her everything I can. The look of frustration changes from anger to pity to sadness, and finally ends in relief. I don't tell her what I needed to talk to Connor about first. I don't want him to hear that from anyone else.

"I'm glad you're okay, but you don't know what Andy did to him, do you?" she asks.

My heart drops to my stomach.

"What do you mean?" I feel tears pricking at my eyes.

"He brought a gun to the office. He would have killed him had Liam not gotten there when he did." Her voice is cold, the fear of losing her brother evident on her face.

"Oh. My. God. Alannah, I'm so sorry. I didn't—" I rush out, but she holds her hand up to stop me.

"It's not me that you need to talk to about this."

I just nod in response. What else is there to say? We sit in silence for a few moments, each of us letting the weight of our revelations sink in. Eventually, we begin chatting about less heavy topics. She tells me about Sean and the dinner they had with his boyfriend. It makes me so happy to see a teenager be so comfortable in sharing that with their family. The stories that Kat told me about when she came out to her parents were heartbreaking. We have a second cup of wine before she heads out.

I sit there with my own thoughts before I grab my phone and do what I should have done weeks ago.

Hadley:

Hey, can I see you?

I set my phone facedown, knowing that he's likely in meetings still, and stand to take the cups to the sink. Before I even get back from the kitchen, I hear my phone notification ding. I walk faster than normal to get to it.

Connor:

I'll come to you. Where are you?

I smile at his response and send my address.

I'm leaving now. Give me ten minutes.

I'm not going anywhere. Don't rush. I know it's further than ten minutes from your office.

I get no response. I start pacing back and forth and decide to call Kat and Ryan. Knowing they're going to lose their shit, I FaceTime them. Ryan picks up first, and after another few seconds Kat answers. I smile at the screen. I love these two so much.

"So, I did something," I say.

Kat is the first to speak. "We'll be there in twenty."

"No! It's nothing bad. I promise. Besides, I'm expecting someone in a few minutes." I smirk when I see Ryan's eyes go wide.

"You didn't?" she squeals.

"Yeah, he said he would be here in ten minutes, and I'm suddenly terrified. I just talked to Alannah. I asked her to come over in case it goes badly. I just wanted to make sure he has his family to support him when he finds out everything." I pause. "Did you guys know that Andy attacked him?"

"He told us, but with everything you were dealing with, we didn't want to add to it." Kat's tone is soft, like she's trying to soothe an angry animal.

"I'm not mad. I was just in shock." I sigh. "How badly did I fuck this up, guys?"

Before either of them can respond, I hear a knock at my door. My heart is beating so loudly, I can hear it.

I quickly say my goodbyes to the girls and sprint to the door, taking a deep, steadying breath before placing my hand on the knob. I pull the door open to see Connor standing there, looking as breathtakingly handsome as ever. I inhale, welcoming his familiar smell of sandalwood and lavender. He's holding two to-go cups from Mud House. His eyes light up when my gaze meets him.

"Mo ghrà." *My love.*

The first words he's said to me in over a month, and oh, how I've missed hearing them. How I needed them while I was stuck in the hell that Andy had created. *My love.*

His love.

Chapter Thirty-Two

Connor

The sight of her nearly knocks me off my feet. When I got her message, I nearly ran out of the shop before Kayleigh yelled at me to take her a coffee too. How that woman remembers her order having only met her once is amazing to me. I'm not convinced she doesn't have superpowers.

"Hi," Hadley says shyly as she steps aside to allow me in.

I walk past her and take in the sparsely-furnished apartment. She doesn't say anything for a moment, and after setting the cups on the makeshift coffee table she has, I pull her to the place she has always belonged: my arms.

"I have missed you so much, mo ghrá." I breathe in her citrusy cinnamon scent.

"I'm so sorry, Connor. I didn't know he attacked you too. I just felt like I needed to heal before you saw me again. It was so bad. Not just him, but what I did too. I'm so sorry. I never meant to hurt you," she rushes out, rambling a mile a minute.

"What do you mean, what you did? Kat and Ryan told me that you were hurt, but they wouldn't tell me anything else or where you were so I could check on you." I raise a brow at her as I pull away to look at her face.

"I feel like I need to preface this with how desperate I was to end the pain he was inflicting. I felt like I had ruined everything with us, and when he told me about your dinner...I don't know. I don't know what I was thinking. It became too much. When he left me on the floor and I came to, barely able to breathe, I just wanted the hurt to go away. I wanted to end it all."

It takes me a moment to fully grasp the weight of her confession. Before I can say anything in response, she's gingerly rolling up her sleeves to show angry red lines up her wrists.

"Oh, mo stór. No." A tear rolls down my cheek. "Are you okay?"

"I am. Well, as okay as I can be. I've been in therapy since. I even went to the house to face what happened, but I'm going to be okay. There is a lot of trauma that he caused, and it's not going to resolve overnight, but I'm getting there." She pauses, as if searching for the words. "I needed to make sure I was in a good place before I reached out to you. I didn't want to put my heaviness and trauma on you. It wouldn't have been fair."

I just stare at her. "Hadley, I love you. Nothing about being away from you for these past weeks has been fair. I just want you. That's all I've wanted since this started."

Her eyes turn glassy with unshed tears as she takes a deep breath. On her exhale, she says, "Táim i ngrá leat."

My eyes don't leave hers for several seconds before I pull her against my chest, my hand tangling in her hair and my lips crashing against hers.

She opens to me instinctively, allowing me in. Our tongues tangle in a sensual dance; I pour all of the emotions of the last six weeks into that kiss. All the heartache, the days of wondering if she was okay. I lift her so she's straddling my lap. The closeness of her body has my skin burning with need. I pull back for a moment, gazing into her eyes again.

"Say it again, mo ghrá," I pant.

"Táim i ngrá leat." She says it so quietly, and it's as if she's breathing life back into my soul.

"Fuck, I love you, Hadley."

I lift her off me, and in one fluid motion she's on her back looking up at me. She squeals at the sudden movement. I give her a devilish smirk as I climb up her body. I press my lips against hers again as I pull down the zipper of her sweatshirt, revealing a tight blue tank top. I stare into her beautiful, soulful eyes as I push the long-sleeved shirt off her shoulders and help her take her arms out without having to sit up.

"Connor," she breathes into me, tangling her fingers into my hair as she pulls me back down to her, our lips finding each other in another fervorous kiss.

The passion her kiss ignites in me has my cock throbbing against the seams of my trousers.

I slide my hand under the tight tank top, pulling it up as I caress her soft skin. I roll a nipple between my thumb and forefinger, working it to a hardened peak. Her soft moans and whimpers send a heatwave straight to my already-stiff cock as I press soft kisses from her lips down to her neck, traveling to her chest, pulling a nipple into my mouth and lightly grazing it with my teeth.

I move inch by inch until I get to her arms, but when I reach her wrists, she tries to pull away. I raise a brow at her, daring her to try to argue with me. Her breath catches as I lower my mouth to her scars, pressing wet kisses against each wrist. I look up into her eyes to see tears streaking her face.

"Beautiful, nothing you could do would push me away," I say before continuing my way down her body.

I have so much time to make up for when it comes to worshiping her stunning, soft frame. I slide my hands down her sides, hooking my fingers into the top of her pants and tugging her jeans down her legs. Exposing her thick thighs, I press a soft kiss to her thong-covered pussy, inhaling the scent I've been longing for weeks for. Her breath catches as I glide my tongue along her center.

"Connor, baby, please. Fuck me," she moans. "It's been too long. I need to feel you inside me."

Ignoring her, I slowly slide the already-soaking tiny scrap of fabric down over her round ass and down her legs. I press my lips against her pelvis, locking eyes with her as I lower my mouth to her soaking cunt. Her breath catches as I dip my tongue into her slit, her moans becoming louder. I slide a finger inside her tight pussy, finding the spot inside her that causes her undoing. I feast on her like she's my last meal as my finger torments her. I feel her contract around me as her body trembles in her release.

Her screams nearly have me prematurely coming in my pants like a teenage boy. I tug my slacks open and pull them down, releasing my erection, the tip coated in a light gleam, evidence of my arousal.

Before she has a chance to fully come down from her climax, I tap my cock against her already-sensitive clit, causing her to buck her hips up toward me. I smirk down at her beautiful body covered in a light sheen of sweat before sliding inside, giving her no time to adjust as I bury myself to the hilt.

I groan at the sensational feeling of her tight channel. Her moans grow louder in protest as I pull out nearly completely just to thrust back inside her, repeating at a steady pace. Her hands claw at my back with each deep plunge. I feel her pussy start to tighten around my cock, and I lean down, crushing my lips against her once more as I drive into her. Her sobs of pleasure are muffled by our kiss as her pussy convulses around me, squeezing me so tight I see stars. My balls tighten for mere seconds before I empty myself inside her.

I pull out, enjoying the sight of my release dripping down her thighs, and press a chaste kiss against her lips before I stand to find a towel to clean us both off. Once I return, I sit her on the couch, pulling her as close to me as I can without sliding inside her again, though my cock is already twitching at the thought.

We sit there for several hours in a comfortable silence, just enjoying one another's presence. I can feel her mind spinning out of control when she takes a deep breath.

"Mo ghrá, what's got the wheels in your mind turning?" I ask as I gently comb my fingers through her hair.

"I don't want to ruin this moment," she says, burying her face in my chest.

"Nothing you say will ruin this moment. What is it?"

She huffs a laugh like she doesn't believe me before she finally responds. "He hasn't signed the papers, and I'm so afraid he will get out. I don't want him to try to hurt you again."

"Between what he did to you and the surveillance footage from the office, there is no way he will walk. I will spend every cent I have to make sure he never gets out."

"Stay with me?" she whispers like she's afraid of my answer.

"You are mine. Never forget that, mo ghrá." I hold her closer to me. "You wouldn't be able to get me out of here if you held a gun to my head."

I chuckle, and she freezes in my arms.

"Too soon, baby," she groans as she cuddles closer into me.

Chapter Thirty-Three

Six months later

Connor and I have been nearly inseparable since our reunion, going back and forth between my tiny apartment and his beautiful home. He's never once complained about the lack of space at my apartment, and even when we're at his place, he's never too far. The only time we're apart is when we have to be at work. I'm finally teaching full time again; the amazing feeling of enriching my students lives makes everything I've been through worth it.

Andy's trial came and went several weeks ago. I chose to testify in the judge's chambers, too afraid to be in the same room and face him. I wasn't scared for myself, though. I knew the officers in the courtroom wouldn't let him attack me. I was worried about what Connor would do that could land him in a cell next to Andy. The sentencing proved to be on my side as well: he was found guilty of two counts of attempted murder. The judge gave him the maximum sentence: twenty years for me and twenty for Connor, to be served consecutively.

I'm sitting in the waiting room of Grove City prison, a forty-minute drive from home on the highway. My lawyer, Danielle Davies, is sitting next to me as we wait to be called back. I know Connor is going to be livid when he finds out, but this is something I need to do alone, not only for myself, but for us. I won't be able to completely move forward until this is done, and Andy has made it abundantly clear that he won't do what I want unless I see him one last time.

A tall, muscular black man with a shiny bald head stands by a metal detector. He calls over to Danielle and me, letting us know that we can come back. I left my purse and phone in her car, so I walk through the metal detector with no issue. Danielle places her briefcase in a bin to go through the x-ray machine and steps through the archway. They take several moments to determine that her briefcase is indeed safe, and after we pass the checkpoint, they finally allow us to continue to the next room.

Danielle goes in first, with me slowly walking in behind her, unsure of what to expect. When I'm finally able to see past her, Andy is sitting at the table, his wrists handcuffed and chained to the table.

He smirks at me as if he's won. Has he not seen where he is?

"Hi, Had. It's been a while." His snarky tone reignites the anger I've been working through with Amy.

Not long enough.

Of course, I don't say that. Not until he does what he said he would.

"I'm here, Andy. What else do you want from me to finish this?" I ask, standing several feet from the table with my arms crossed against my chest in a protective stance.

"I just wanted to see you. Mom said your weak ass couldn't even finish what I started."

His dark chuckle turns my stomach. I guess the façade I fell in love with once upon a time has truly disappeared entirely.

"I guess not. Is that all?" I ask as calmly as I can manage, not bothering to argue. Yet.

Danielle slides the divorce paper toward him. He looks up, his gaze meeting mine. He picks up the pen and places it to the paper, but he pauses.

"Just remember, one day I will get out of here, and no matter where you are, I will finish what I started," he snarls as he signs his name with a flourish and slides the papers back to Danielle, who promptly places them in her bag and steps back, nodding at me.

That's all the cue I need.

"Honestly, I'd like to see you try. I may have had a weak moment and tried to end the pain *you've* caused me, but I am *not* that weak woman anymore. I will never allow anyone, especially not you, to touch me in such a way again for as long as I live. I will especially not allow you to try to ruin what I've found."

I pause briefly to allow my words to sink in.

"Though I guess I should thank you for that. Had you not pushed me to see it your way and have a 'well-rounded life experience,' I wouldn't have met Connor." I repeat his words from our anniversary to him, satisfaction and pride making me stand a little taller.

"You whore! You're still fucking him?" Andy's snarl makes me chuckle to myself.

I don't bother responding, just give Danielle a nod as I walk toward the door. We leave him sitting there, throwing insults after us. I breathe a sigh of relief once we're back to the waiting room we had been forced to sit in for over an hour before seeing my now ex-husband.

"How do you feel?" Danielle asks as she guides me toward the exit.

"Like I want to go to my man and tell him I'm finally free." My cheeks hurt from the wide smile that takes over my face. "Let's get out of here." I open the passenger side of the car and slide in.

We're heading down Gilmore Avenue on our way toward the highway when I see a familiar coffee shop. I ask Danielle to pull over so I can grab a quick cup, and if I'm honest, I'd like to see the moose painting at this one. I smile at the memory of the conversation I had with Kayleigh so many months ago.

Danielle parks right in front and allows me to get out and walk inside. I offer to get her a cup, but she declines and says she's going to check her email while I'm getting coffee. When I walk in, I see Kayleigh behind the counter.

When she sees me, she scoots around quickly and walks toward me, wrapping me in a hug. "I am so happy to see you! We were worried about you."

I freeze. What does she know?

"Um, thanks?" I pat her back.

She steps back and giggles.

"I'm sorry. Connor has become close with Liam after...everything that's happened." I see a small shudder shake her body. "We both have. Connor has made it a point to stop by Mud House daily. Jill manages that location now, and she's said he has become an honorary opening employee. Always there as she comes in for the day. He scared the shit out of me when I opened for her a while back."

"Yeah, he didn't sleep well when I was..." I pause, unsure how to finish my thought. "Healing."

She simply nods in response, walking back behind the counter to get me a cup of coffee, the peppermint mocha latte that I had before. I love that she has this year-round, not just during the holidays like other coffee places. She crosses the distance between us, handing me the drink. I try to give her my card to pay, and she raises her brow at me.

"Absolutely not. This one is on me. Don't be a stranger from now on. I'll be at my shop in Central Falls at least twice a week. I expect to see you there." She winks at me.

"Thank you."

I adore how kind this woman is. I hope Liam knows how lucky he is.

I turn to leave when a beautiful woman comes to a halt behind me. "Whoa there, Silver Fox. I may adore how Kay and Liam met, but it looked painful. I'd rather not experience it myself."

I hear Kayleigh giggling behind me and turn my head to face her, the question on my face.

"Oh, I'll tell you all about that when you come visit me tomorrow. Jana, leave Hadley alone." She rolls her eyes and goes to the next customer waiting in line.

Jana looks me up and down with a devilish smirk before waving her fingers in the air at me to say goodbye. I make my way back to Danielle's car to find her on the phone with another client. I was in there longer than I anticipated, but she says nothing, just smiles as she takes off for home. I pull my phone out, turning it back on to a flurry of text messages.

Connor:

> I miss you already, beautiful.

Kat:

> Babe, what happened? We're dying here.

Ryan:

> Woman, you need to get back to us. He's asking why you're not answering his texts.

Connor:

> Mo ghrá, are you okay?

Shit, I should have left my phone with them to respond to him. I send responses to everyone, starting with Connor.

Hadley:

> I miss you too, baby. More than you know. Are you still at the office?

Hadley:

> I just sent him a message. It's done. I need to see him, then I'll call you two later.

Connor's response comes in as I'm typing the message to the group chat.

Connor:

> Yes, I'm at the office. About to go into a meeting. Is everything OK? I was starting to panic when you didn't respond. The girls said your phone died.

I don't respond. I just turn to Danielle.

"Can you drop me off at Connor's office?"

Her knowing smile is the only reply I need.

Chapter Thirty-Four

Connor

The door to my office is closed as Gina and I are going over the latest contracts that the sales team have been working to bring in for the current quarter. Gina has everything laid out as usual, confirming numbers before she finalizes what is to be sent to the clients.

"Unless there is something else we need to discuss, I've got plans this evening, so I'm heading out early." Gina smirks as she gathers her things.

"Have a good night," I chuckle.

Knowing her, she's going to go home and watch *The Bachelor*.

She stands to leave when my office door swings open. Jordan is standing there with a sly smile on his face. I raise my brow at him in question, and his grin grows even wider. Gina waves goodbye and walks past us both.

"What is it, Jordan?" I ask since he hasn't replied to my clearly questioning eyebrow.

"You have a visitor, boss." He moves aside to reveal Hadley.

My heart pounds in my chest as I take in the sight. She's dressed in a short-sleeved low-cut t-shirt and a pair of dark jeans. The outfit is so form-fitting, it clings to her curves, making my dick twitch, knowing she's all mine. What I wouldn't give to bend her over my desk and rail her into next week.

"Beautiful, I wasn't expecting you today." I smile at her as I cross the distance, crashing my mouth against hers.

I don't care that my assistant is still standing only a few feet away from us. I pull her perfect form flush against my body, and she melts into me. Her lips part, allowing my tongue to explore her mouth. We cling to one another for several moments before Jordan clears his throat, tearing us out of our bubble. I growl as I pull away, both of us panting. I glare up at Jordan, waiting to see what was so important that he felt the need to interrupt us.

"Boss, you have a meeting with Mr. Asher in thirty minutes..." It's a question, not a statement.

"Give me five minutes," I respond, nodding my head toward the door in a *get the fuck out* gesture.

He seems to understand my nonverbal cue, and I hear the quiet chuckle he's trying to stifle as he walks out.

I turn back to Hadley and smile at her. "To what do I owe the pleasure of this visit, my love?"

She pulls me in for a tight hug before she looks up at me, her beautiful face becoming serious. "Danielle and I just went to see Andy."

I stiffen at the statement, and she continues quickly.

"I didn't tell you because I needed to face him one last time on my own. Plus, it was the only way he'd do what I've been asking."

She pulls a packet of paper out of her bag and hands it to me.

"What is this?" I ask, ignoring the confession.

She seems to be alright, so I can't be too upset that she did something to aid in her healing process. I take the papers, looking over the pages in my hand. At the top, I see *Divorce Decree*.

My eyes dart back up to hers. "Are you serious?"

Hadley's eyes are glassy with unshed tears as she nods. "I didn't want to get your hopes up in case he decided not to sign."

"A mhuirnín." My arms wrap tightly around her as I inhale, committing everything in this moment to memory. "I love you so much."

I wake up to an empty bed, the clock reading seven in the morning. I groan as I stretch my limbs, scrubbing a hand down my face. Cocking my head, I hear faint sounds coming from the other side of the house. Pulling on my flannel pants and a black t-shirt, I pad out of the bedroom and into the hall.

As I near the main part of the house, I can hear Hadley whispering, but I can't make out who she's speaking to. I turn the corner to see Hadley, my family, and our friends in my kitchen, none the wiser to my entrance. Liam sees me first and winks before he clears his throat.

Everyone turns towards me and screams, "HAPPY BIRTHDAY!"

Hadley has the brightest smile on her face, and Sean comes running toward me and wraps his arms around my torso.

"Happy birthday, Uncle," he says as he does the flashy hand movement Sean Hayes does in *Will and Grace* during all of his "Just Jack" bits.

I bite back a laugh, shaking my head at him, when I notice James standing behind him. I walk over to him, wrapping him in a hug as well.

"It's good to see you, kid." I smile down at him.

He gives me a grin in response.

"Thank you, everyone. This is so unexpected." I chuckle as I walk toward Hadley. "This was you, wasn't it?" I ask her pointedly.

She doesn't speak, just stands on the tips of her toes, pressing her lips to mine. I wrap my arms around her waist, pulling her to me. It takes all my restraint not to pick her up and lay her out on the table right now, my morning wood barely concealed under the plaid print of my pants. She looks perfect in the loose crop top she has on, her breasts barely hidden. I love the confidence she has in her body, that she doesn't hide her beauty. She truly is the most gorgeous woman I've ever seen.

"I figured it would be the second-best gift I could give you for your birthday." She winks at me.

I press my lips to her ear. "I don't care who is here. I *will* toss you over my shoulder, take you to our room, and make you scream so loudly everyone on this continent will know when you strangle my cock as you come."

She shudders in my arms, a beautiful pink blush creeping up her neck.

"Later, baby." She walks away from me and over to her friends, and I think I detect a little extra sway in her hips.

It's good to see Kayleigh and Jana here too. Looking to my left, I see Alannah.

"Baby sister." I pull her in for a hug before she turns to go talk to the girls.

Then I walk to Liam, who's leaning against the wall, hands shoved in his jean pockets.

"Good to see you smiling, friend."

"It is, isn't it? Where are the kids? Joel and Lance didn't come?" I ask as I look around my kitchen at our mix of friends and family.

"They took the kids to Lance's mom's. She's so great with them, but Daisey was pissed she wasn't going to see you. She told Kay that she will never forgive her for not letting her see her boyfriend." He chuckles.

His and Kayleigh's adorable three-year-old daughter has become my shadow whenever I'm around, and I can't even be mad about it because she so damn cute.

"I guess I'll have to stop by one day next week when she's at Mud House and spend some time with her so she will forgive you both, huh?" I respond with a laugh.

"I'm sure she'd love that." He nods once, clapping a hand on my shoulder.

We sit around the dining room table and feast on an amazing breakfast Hadley and Alannah made while I was asleep. Kayleigh brought an assortment of pastries that I'm having difficulty sharing, and the morning goes by too quickly with all the people I'm closest to.

Liam and I spend the rest of the day chatting in my den while the women in our lives are holed up somewhere nearby, talking amongst themselves. I'm about to ask Liam's opinion on something I have been contemplating for a while when we hear Kat ask Kayleigh a question.

"Spill it, sister. Why do you call him Cap?"

Liam starts chuckling, and his face turns red. I raise a brow at him in question, and he jerks his head toward where the women are, so we stand and follow the sound of their voices to hear not Kayleigh, but Jana, telling the story about how Liam became Cap.

Chapter Thirty-Five

One and a half years ago

I walk out of the elevator and onto the floor where my desk resides at DL Technologies to see a woman with the longest legs and perkiest tits I've ever seen. My cock twitches in my pants instantly.

I've always had a healthy sex life with Hadley, but *damn*. This woman has me ready to make a mess of myself in my pants just at the sight of her.

I stroll toward the mystery woman to find her speaking with the head of HR, June, who is showing her around. Apparently, it's her first day at DL.

And what a lucky day for me.

June receives a call on her cell and steps away as I squeeze in beside her, placing my things on my desk. I turn toward her, my best lopsided smirk pulling at my lips.

"Hey there. I'm Andy. It looks like we're going to be desk buddies," I say with a wink. My deep voice is smooth as I speak to her.

I know I can lay on the charm when I need to, but this is something different.

"Hi! I'm Naomi. It's so great to meet you." She smiles brightly at me. "I've been told you'll be training me, actually."

"Great, I'll show ya the ropes once we can ditch June." I hitch my thumb over my shoulder, a playful grin spreading on my face.

I wonder if she'd let me use ropes on her.

I shake the thought from my mind. I'm married, for Christ's sake.

Hanging up her call, June walks over and introduces Naomi and me, as if we haven't just been chatting. Satisfied that her job is done, June walks away, leaving me to take over.

Mm, I'd love nothing more.

We spend that first month pussyfooting around our attraction until one morning, she comes in, obviously suffering from a terrible lack of sleep. Seeing the deep purple rings below her gorgeous eyes, I ask her what's wrong. Wiping her cheek with the back of her hand, she tells me she is struggling and will be putting in her notice as soon as she finds a new job.

"Why the fuck would you leave me?" I seethe.

"What do you mean, leave you? You're married, Andy! These feelings that have developed aren't going away. I need to separate myself from this entire thing," she whispers vehemently. "I want more than you can give me."

I pull her into the closest room with a solid door, flipping on the switch when the door is firmly shut. As soon as I see her tear-streaked face, I cup her cheeks in my hands and pull her face toward mine, crashing my lips against hers, tasting the saltiness of her tears as I finally give in to what I have been craving since the moment I met this sinfully beautiful woman.

And my God, sin has never tasted so good.

It's been the most enthralling seven months of my life. Naomi is a fire-cracker, and the things she lets me do to her...fuck, I'm constantly hard just at the memory of her tight little body wrapped around me. Thinking about how her perfectly perky tits bounced as I fucked her into oblivion last night before I went home has me aching in need.

Hadley doesn't suspect a thing. We've even started talking about hav-ing kids. I've been faking my orgasms with her since I met Naomi. The only way I can even stay hard long enough to get her off is if I have her bent over so I can't see her face. I just close my eyes and pretend she is Naomi.

Not that she compares to my perfect temptress. Hadley could never be enough for me now that I've tasted what true pleasure is, and it's wrapped up in a blonde bombshell that is constantly ready for me to fill her needy cunt. Their bodies are complete opposites; Hadley is thick and has some curves, but Naomi is tight and smooth in all the right places.

The number of times Naomi has allowed me to get rough with her has opened up a side of me I've had to keep hidden for so long. I've always worn a mask around others, and it left me feeling so unfulfilled. Naomi lets me dominate her, use her however I want, and she always begs for more.

The only reason I haven't left Hadley is because of the prenup. Stupidest fucking thing I ever did. I'd lose my inheritance from my parents if they knew. I want to fill Naomi's cunt until she's swollen with my baby. Still, even with as much as I get paid at DL, I wouldn't be able to take care of Naomi the way I need to once she's carrying my child. She's going to look so good with a round stomach, showing the world exactly who she belongs to. I bet her tits will get even bigger too.

My dick twitches at the thought.

Naomi has made it clear that if she doesn't get more time with me, I'm going to lose her. And if I want to see our baby, I have to find a way. She's a month into her pregnancy today, which is, ironically, my anniversary with Hadley.

I've felt no remorse about my relationship with Naomi until today. Hadley is sweet, but such a fucking pushover. She'll do anything for me, and honestly, it's pretty damn pathetic. Naomi pushes me and lets me put my hands on her in a way I have always craved. I don't have to mask my anger, the darkest parts of myself, with her.

My eyes nearly roll into the back of my head when I see Jim standing in the parking lot of Providence. Hadley will spend an hour talking to him if I let her.

I step away once I'm out of the car while she speaks with Jim. Pulling out my phone, I send a message to Naomi.

Hey, sexy. We just got here, but she won't stop talking to this damn valet. I'll let you know when it's done. I can't wait to be able to spend every night nailing you and not have to leave until morning.

Hurry up, babe! I miss you already! My wrists are feeling bare, not being wrapped with your tie. (wink emoji)

I smile at the response.

I'll have to give her tonight, but then I'll start to move my clothes to your place slowly. Fuck, sexy, I can't wait to keep you tied up all night and keep you full of me whenever I want.

Finally growing annoyed at having to wait to get this over with so I can be with my firecracker, I stroll as calmly as I can muster to where Jim and Hadley are standing and place my hand on the small of her back to guide her inside. I hate this gentle romantic bullshit that she likes. But I guess if one little gesture keeps me in her good graces long enough to get through the required time before the clause in our prenup expires, it's worth it. I don't want her to have that money. She *can't* have that money.

Once we're seated, Hadley attempts small talk, which I'm just not interested in. I'm over this evening and just want to go to Naomi's and sink my dick into her.

"Listen, we need to talk." I feel the tension rising in my chest, unsure of what to expect from her.

"Okay," she all but whispers in response.

Here we go. Time to put on a show.

"I love you, Had. I will love you forever, but I'm not really happy. I haven't been for a while," I say with a huff.

"You're leaving me?" she sobs.

Her face falls and her eyes land on the floor, and honestly, I'm not mad that she refuses to make eye contact.

"What? No."

Shit, I did this all wrong. I'm going to lose the money and Naomi. I have to pull this off.

I shake my head and pull her into a hug. "I don't want to leave you. I just want to experience..."

I pause. How can I say this without her costing me everything?

"More."

"I don't understand." She trembles in my arms. "What more could you want to experience?"

I choke down a laugh. Oh, if this stupid bitch only knew what I would do to her if given the chance.

"I need more in bed. There is just so much more to explore than what you can provide me." I drag in a quick breath, holding back from cracking my hand against her ass for being so fucking naïve. "I told you, I love you. You can't tell me you're satisfied."

I can't believe she's dating my fucking boss. How the fuck did that even happen? A month ago, she told me she went on a date, but hasn't mentioned anything since.

Maybe I shouldn't have been ignoring her calls and texts, but my life has been too good with Naomi to bother with her. She's serving her purpose, staying the hell away from me while I thrive with my bombshell and our little grenade inside her.

I need to find a way to get shit back on track so I don't lose what is mine. Or what Naomi wants. Fuck me, the number of things she's already bought for the baby would have me on edge if I didn't make the money I do. We need the trust to keep living this lifestyle if Naomi wants to stay home with our little girl. I've got to get Hadley to stick around just for a few more months. Then I'll have everything I want.

I walk into the office of one of my closest friends, Johnny, who also happens to be my lawyer. He's known Hadley and me for years. He's never really gotten close to her, though she's tried to befriend him. I think that's why I became so close to him. He doesn't give a shit about how nice and sweet she is and seems to barely tolerate her most of the time.

Jesus, I can't believe I stayed with Hadley as long as I did, even before I met Naomi. Ever since I have been able to be the real me, just looking at Hadley disgusts me. She is so weak, so...soft. She never would have been able to satisfy me. Our end was inevitable.

So, when I decided to update my will after Hadley and I's...disagreement...I wanted to make sure he had all the information. I want to see his face when I tell him what I'm planning when I do end up kicking rocks. With as much as he doesn't like my wife, I figure he'll get a kick out of it.

"Man, what the hell happened to your hands?" Johnny says as soon as he sees me walk in taking a sip of my coffee.

"It's fine. I just had to knock some sense into Hadley," I snicker.

"What?" His cold tone confuses me, his face taking on an almost angry look.

"She decided to grow a backbone when she found out that I knocked up Naomi. She'll be fine." I shrug my shoulders. "I set up a signal jammer until I could get her phone, so she won't be causing trouble for us."

"How can I help you, Andy?" he asks, his tone serious.

"You know I can't divorce the bitch because of the money. It's something Naomi is pushing me for. As soon as she found out about the trust, she pushed me to stay with Hadley until the clause my parents put in the prenup was completed." I blow out a breath. "So I want to make sure that I get the last word if my time comes before I get to leave Hadley behind for good."

I leave Johnny's office several hours later, satisfied once everything has been finalized. I head straight for my car and pull the semi-automatic pistol I purchased from the pawn shop out of the glove box. I'm ready to get the rest of my day over with now that Hadley and Naomi have been taken care of. It's time to deal with Connor Quinn.

I hear his voice before I see him. Jordan has stepped away to go to the bathroom when I walk up to Connor's office. I stroll calmly to his door and knock softly so as not to give myself away.

"Come in," his voice booms from within the office.

God, he's such a dick. I am really going to enjoy this.

I take a step forward and slowly push the door open to reveal Connor sitting behind his desk.

Here we go.

"Connor," I say dryly with a grin plastered on my face.

"How may I help you, Andy?" His brow raises in question.

"I'm just amused that you claimed you were *so* into my wife, yet you had some special dinner last night." I let out a loud snort.

We continue the conversation, which is a means to an end for me. Or for him, if I think about it. Eventually, I've had enough and say what I came to say.

"Just stop contacting my wife. She told you we're together now." I let my perfectly crafted mask drop as a smile that would make Michael Myers tremble in fear pulls at my lips.

"That's Hadley's choice to make. She's an adult, and she can tell me if she doesn't want my friendship." His body goes rigid with the statement.

"No, it's *my* choice." I wink at him.

It's time for this to end. For *him* to end, so I can keep her with me for just a few more months and get the money to allow Naomi and I to start over wherever she wants. I pull the gun from under my jacket and raise it to his eye level. He continues speaking, trying to talk me down.

"Andy, this isn't necessary." His voice is full of panic.

"What isn't necessary is that you are fucking my wife, Connor. I don't give a shit who you are. Just because I'm fucking someone else doesn't mean I actually expected her to go out and slip into someone else's bed. The bitch is *mine*," I growl.

"If you're going to shoot me for being with Hadley, then do it, because I wouldn't change a damn thing. She means the world to me, but you will *not* talk about her in a derogatory way."

"Let's see if you really feel like you have a leg to stand on after this." I lower the gun, aiming toward his leg just to see if he'll fall when I squeeze the trigger.

Before I have a chance to shoot, I'm hit from the side by what feels like a damn wrecking ball, forcing me onto the ground. My gun flies out of my hands as I hit the floor.

I've been in this hellhole for six fucking months. Hadley had the balls to visit me yesterday to sign the divorce papers. I gave in to her, knowing I won't get out of here after the dumb cunt tried to kill herself and blamed it on me and not her own weakness. Plus, that pussy Connor filed charges against me too.

I need to hit someone. It needs to be on them, though, or the guards will send me back to the SHU. It's too fucking quiet there.

Jesus, I'm losing my fucking mind.

I see Miles walk toward me and smile to myself.

"Pussy, get the fuck out of here," I taunt.

He throws the first punch, and it's game on. I swing back at him, landing a jab against the right side of his jaw. Before I can pull back for another swing, I feel something grab me under my arms, holding me back. I struggle against whoever it is.

Marcus stands, and a smug grin crosses his face. "You make this shit too easy, you dumb cunt."

He says nothing else before stomping hard on my right ankle. The pain shoots up my leg, and I let out a loud groan.

"You fucker! Do you really think that's going to stop me? I will kill you for this. I don't care if I have to spend a month in the SHU. I will end you," I spit.

Before I can continue my threats, his foot comes down on my other ankle.

"FUCK!" I scream.

"I have a message for you," he taunts. "Mr. Lewis wanted you to know that all of this is for Hadley. He never acted on his true feelings for her. Now it's too late. He won't let you get away with it, though."

His smile becomes menacing, evil.

"Now go down like a good boy and fuck all the way off," he snarls as a sharp pain sears across my abdomen.

They continue stabbing me with a fucking shank for what feels like hours. The pain is so bad, it feels like I'm burning alive.

Fuck! Is this how Hadley felt? What about Naomi?

She enjoyed it, though. She begged for it.

Fuck, it's so cold. I can't open my eyes. It hurts too bad.

I wish I had killed Hadley. If she had just died, I wouldn't be here. I would still be with Naomi. But she had to go and fuck that up too.

Fuck, she's going to be so mad when she sees the letter. Though it will break Hadley.

Shit, what about my baby girl? I'll never get to see her grow up.

Fuck, it's cold.

Voices shouting in the distance get closer to wherever I am. I can't make out what they're saying.

Why can't I warm up?

If I get out of this, I will find a way to end Hadley once and for all. Stupid bitch.

Chapter Thirty-Six

I jolt upright in bed as my phone rings on the bedside table next to me. Connor grumbles in his sleep, trying to pull me back to him. I reach to the table to see Danielle is calling me and notice that it's nearly two a.m.

"Danielle? Is everything okay?" My voice is groggy with sleep, my brain still trying to wake up.

"I'm afraid not. I have some news that couldn't wait." She sounds unsure as she speaks.

"It's two in the morning. What is so important that it couldn't possibly wait a few more hours?" I grumble.

"It's Andy." Danielle's pause has my stomach in my throat. "He was attacked this afternoon, shortly after we left. I just got the call, Hadley. He didn't make it."

"What?!" I scream.

Connor flies upright, looking around and trying to figure out what I'm yelling for. I clutch his thigh as tears start to fall down my cheeks.

"What do you mean, he didn't make it? He was killed? What the fuck happened?"

"They said he was starting shit all day and one of the inmates had enough of it." She takes a breath, allowing me to take in the information she's shared. "He was stabbed with a handmade shank."

I'm trembling, trying to control my breathing so I don't pass out or vomit.

"He was found in an empty corridor that had no surveillance cameras." She sighs. "They didn't find him until an hour after the final count. They said he bled out."

I feel another scream working its way up my throat.

"The tough part of this is that you aren't divorced. Since you still have the paperwork because you wanted to show Connor, it hasn't been filed yet. Hadley, you're now a widow, so we're going to have to discuss what that means."

The scream dissipates in the wave of pure shock. Yesterday was such an amazing day. Why does he get to ruin that? I think I mutter a thanks before disconnecting the call.

"Mo ghrá, whatever you need, say the word. I'm here." Connor is there, his arms around me, holding me in comfort.

My heart is shattered, but not because of any love for Andy. That's long gone, but the memories of who he was remain. Knowing the man he once was, and knowing he will never be that man ever again. I really had hoped he would find himself again while he was locked up. I shudder. His poor parents; they won't survive this.

I bury my face in Connor's chest, sobs wracking my body. He doesn't say anything, just holds me. Eventually, we lie back down. He holds me tight, running his fingers through my hair, helping me relax until I end up asleep wrapped around him.

The past week has gone by incredibly fast. I've had to meet with so many lawyers, and I've been in constant communication with Andy's parents. They informed me this morning that I needed to be at the reading of his will. Connor has been by my side every step of the way—my rock, never wavering in his endless support—and I'm so thankful for him.

I know it's been hard for him after what Andy did to both of us. He doesn't know the full extent of my injuries, but he knows what it caused me to do. I also know Kat and Ryan have been pestering him to keep an eye on me. They're afraid I'm going to break. I've been reaching out to Amy to process my feelings, so I'm taking care of myself. I refuse to let Andy take anything else from me, not even in death.

We're all sitting in a small conference room: Andy's parents, the lawyers, Connor, myself, and the executor of his will, Naomi. I shouldn't be shocked that she's here. She's had his child, after all. We are all sitting around a long table in Andy's lawyer's office. Naomi attempts to start speaking, but he abruptly interrupts her.

"Mr. and Mrs. James. Hadley," Mr. Lewis says, looking between the three of us. "I know this is highly inappropriate; however, I can't sit here and allow this to go on this way." He pauses, glancing at me with sympathy in his eyes. "If it's okay with you, *I* would like to be the one to read the will."

Mr. James says a quiet "yes" while I nod in agreement. Mr. Lewis begins reading while Naomi sniffles from across the table.

I sit in a daze, leaning into Connor. This entire day has been a clusterfuck. Andy left me everything but the house, which he left to Naomi and their child. He left a letter that he had wanted Naomi, of all people, to read to me. Mr. Lewis squashes that so fast, my head nearly spins. The letter includes details of when their affair began and a weak apology to me, only to change his tune in the next words to inform me that I am the worst thing that ever happened to him. That I am and always will be nothing in comparison to Naomi. It continues with more hateful words that even have Naomi cringing in her seat.

As Connor and I stand to leave, Mr. Lewis intercepts us. "May I have a word, Hadley?"

"Sure, but Connor isn't going anywhere."

My response surprises him, and he raises a brow at me. "Are you sure you want him here for *all* of the details?"

"He knows what Andy did, and I'm not hiding anything from him," I clarify.

Connor wraps an arm around my waist in solidarity, holding me tight against him.

"Okay. I just wanted to let you know, off the record..." He glances around to make sure no one is within earshot. "He did suffer. When I spoke to the warden, they said he didn't stop breathing until five minutes *after* they found him. The number of wounds couldn't be determined at first glance."

A devilish smile crosses his face as he continues.

"The inmate who confessed told them he had broken Andy's ankles before repeatedly stabbing him. Andy was left slowly bleeding out for forty-five minutes before the last count. With the confession, they won't do an autopsy unless you push for it, since you were technically still married."

Connor stiffens at the information, but I don't respond, instead just nodding and pulling Connor closer to me. We walk out of the room and head out to the Tesla. I'm in such a daze after what just happened, I don't even realize that we've made it back to Connor's house until he parks and opens my door to help me out.

"Mo ghrá, what do you need?" He pulls me into him as I stand from the passenger seat.

"I don't know." I sigh. "Is it wrong that I'm thankful he's gone and he can't hurt anyone else? Does that make me a bad person?" I bite my bottom lip. "I was honestly more worried about Naomi and her baby. I can't imagine what was going through his mind."

"It's not wrong, my love. You just need time to process. Let me know what I can do to help, okay? Don't try to go it alone. Remember I'm here." He wraps me in a tight embrace and presses his lips to my temple.

I haven't shed any tears since I received the phone call that night, but something about this moment allows my emotions to break free of the wall I had been keeping them locked behind.

"Just hold me? Please?" I whisper into his chest.

Without a word, he lifts me into his arms and carries me to his bed. We lie there together in silence until the tears dry and darkness pulls me into unconsciousness.

Several hours later, I wake up to the doorbell. Connor gently untangles me from his warmth, and I sit up.

"Who is it?" I ask, my voice coated in sleep.

"It's Amy. I texted and asked her to come by. It's okay if you don't want to talk about it. I just wanted her close so you can have as much support as you need."

His gentle smile elicits another round of tears. This time, though, they're tears of joy and relief.

"Thank you." I pull off the covers and stand from the bed, walking to him and jumping into his arms. "Thank you for taking care of me like you do. I love you so much."

Our lips find each other for a quick kiss before he sets me down to answer the door.

"I love you. I'll show you just how much later." He smirks over his shoulder, making me giggle.

Chapter Thirty-Seven

Connor

I rush to the door before I take advantage of a shitty situation just to make her feel better physically. I adjust my dick in my pants before welcoming Amy into my home. That's the last thing she needs to see.

"Hey. She'll be out in a minute. She just woke up." I motion for her to come in.

I lead Amy to the living room, where she makes herself comfortable in my armchair, strategically leaving the couch empty for Hadley and me.

Hadley comes out to the living room, her hair braided at the nape of her neck. She's changed into a pair of yoga pants and one of my sweatshirts, making me smile. I love seeing her in my clothes; it fuels this primal, possessive part of me that has claimed her as my own.

I pull her into my arms and press another quick kiss to her lips. "I'll let you two talk. Let me know if you need anything."

"Stay?" She looks at me through her lashes. "Please?"

I simply nod and sit next to her on the couch. She's leaning into my side, so I wrap my arm around her, pulling her in tight.

Amy clears her throat. "So, tell me how you're feeling."

Hadley takes in a deep breath before blowing it out. "I feel like a weight has been lifted off of my shoulders." I feel her relax even more into me with the statement. "We got a lot of detail about what happened from his lawyer, so that's still sinking in, but I feel relieved. I didn't believe his torment would end if he ever got out, so I can breathe again."

"That's good that you're not holding on to any feelings of guilt. You have really grown so much, but I think both Connor and I are worried that with this happening, it could lead you down a dark path again that no one wants to see you take." Amy's gentle tone gives voice to my fear without judgment.

"I know, and I'd be lying if I said I wasn't worried." Hadley's smile is weak. "I know you and I have had this conversation before. I can only control how I react to a situation." She pauses for a brief moment before she pulls my gaze to hers. "I feel content, though. With my life, with where I am emotionally, spiritually, and physically. And with you. With *us*."

"Tá mé i ngrá leat. Irrevocably and beyond words." A rogue tear trails down my face as I press my lips to her temple.

"Tá mé i ngrá leat," she repeats to me her eyes glistening with unshed tears.

"Well, now that we've gotten that out of the way. May I speak freely?" Amy chimes in, pulling us out of each other.

An infectious giggle erupts from Hadley's chest. "Always."

"I can't tell you how happy I was when Connor called me with the news. The douche canoe deserved what he got." A wide grin splits across her face as she leans forward and pats Hadley's leg.

Chapter Thirty Eight

Connor

Two months later

I pull up outside my house and see Hadley and Alannah standing out front. Alannah looks like she's about to leave when they both notice me.

"Sister, what are you doing here?" I smile as I walk over to her, wrapping her in a tight embrace before releasing her and stepping toward Hadley. "Mo ghrá."

I press my lips against hers, savoring her soft lips as she melts into me with a soft whimper.

"Ew, brother. I am still here," Alannah groans, pretending to gag.

"Tá brón orm," I chuckle. "So, what are you doing here?"

"Sorry, brother. She's become one of my best friends. You shouldn't be dating someone so awesome if you didn't want me to stop by unexpectedly so often."

Hadley chuckles. "I love you too, Lan."

"I've got to go. I'm taking Sean and James to dinner." My baby sister winks at me before she leaves. Such a smartass.

"Are you ready to go to dinner?" I ask Hadley, pulling her in for another kiss, this one not so rushed.

I press my lips to hers, swiping my tongue across her lower lip. She gasps, opening to me when I grab her ass, lifting her into my arms. Her legs tangle around my waist, and I grip her hair to keep control. I swipe my tongue past her lips, getting lost in the feeling of her tongue swirling around mine, as though we're both determined to make this moment last. My cock pulses in need at the feeling of her against me. The way she expertly teases me, tugging on my hair all the while, kissing me like it's what gives her breath.

I pull away, breaking the kiss, leaving us both panting.

"Beautiful girl, if we don't go to dinner right now, I'm going to take you inside and fuck you on every single surface that we have yet to christen," I growl, my arousal poking into her center while she's still wrapped around me.

"As much as we'd both enjoy that, let's save it for later. I'm hungry." Her lips twitch in a playful smile. She's planning something.

I groan inwardly. "Let's get out of here so we can get back home sooner rather than later and I can have my dessert."

I grin at her as she slides down my body. The friction of the motion has me groaning again.

"Woman, you will be the death of me."

We pull up to Providence about twenty minutes later, my dick still throbbing in my pants. Fuck me, I can't wait to get her home. There is something very important I need to do first, though. The last time she was here is tainted with a memory that I don't want her to hold on to. I know she's missed Jim, so I want to be here with her, to help her make a new memory.

We step out of the car, and Jim is there to greet us. He shakes my hand when he recognizes me, then immediately turns his attention to Hadley, his whole face brightening as if the sun just came out from behind the clouds.

"My sweet girl. How are you doing?" His gentle voice has her eyes glistening. "I'm glad to see the two of you tonight. Your favorite is on the special board."

This man adores Hadley, and just witnessing it has me respecting him on another level. The three of us chat for a while before we finally head inside. She clutches my arm as we walk through the door.

"Thank you for doing this, baby." Her soft voice is barely audible.

"Beautiful, I would do anything for you."

Once seated, I order a bottle of wine for us to share. Her eyes light up when she sees that the shrimp risotto is in fact on the menu.

"This really is my favorite." Her face beams with a smile that could light up the room.

We sit and simply enjoy one another's company, chatting about our days. She tells me about Ryan's latest dating disaster. While I enjoy tormenting her most of the time about her tragic dating experiences, she and Kat have become like adopted little sisters to me. They deserve the world with as much as they've done for me. Bringing my girl back to me is a debt that no amount of money can repay.

Once we've finished dinner, I pull her chair closer to me, not giving a shite if I bring attention to us.

"There is something I wanted to talk to you about tonight. I wanted to do it here so that the memories you have here can start to become happy again." I gently brush her hair out of her eyes and tuck it behind her ear so I can see her face. "Mo ghrá, move in with me?"

A mixture of shock and pure joy takes over her expression.

"Really?" she questions, her confidence from this afternoon faltering.

"Mo ghrá, we're together whenever we're not working, we have keys to each other's places." I pause, seeing her process my words. "Live with me. I want my home to be *our* home. If you don't like my house, we can buy another one. So long as you say you'll be with me. Wherever you are is my home."

One year later

"Baby! We're gonna be late! Daisey is going to be so mad if we aren't there before the cake!" I shout toward Connor's office.

"Mo stór, we still have an hour before we need to be there."

He snickers as he strolls toward me, his strong arms wrapping around my waist as he pulls me in.

"I promised her we'd be the first to arrive, and we will be." His brogue is thick with desire as he runs his nose from my ear to my throat, sending shivers through my body.

"Babe, don't start something we don't have time to finish," I moan into his neck.

The dark chuckle that escapes his lips has heat pooling in my core. Damn, this man does things to me I can't explain. I groan as he guides me backward toward the wall. He has me caged in, his lips against my mouth, spreading me open for him. He dips his tongue in, tangling around mine.

The way he knows how to elicit a reaction from my body when I'm trying my damnedest to behave is maddening. I moan into his mouth when I feel the stiffness of his length pressing against my core.

"Babe," I pant as he pulls away.

A wicked glint lights in his eye as his hands glide over my body, working me over like only he has ever been able to. His lips press against my collarbone while his hands are cupping my breasts through my dress. He tugs at the neckline, exposing me to the cool air surrounding us. He rolls my peaked nipples between his expert fingers, tweaking the hard buds and adding just enough pain to have me writhing against him.

He drops to his knees, his mouth pressing kisses in a trail down my soft stomach. I gasp when his hands roam under my dress, dragging my panties over my hips and down my full thighs before they're completely gone and in his pocket. That wicked glint hasn't left his eyes as he dips his head and disappears under my dress, lifting my legs so they're on his shoulders, bracing me against the wall.

"Christ, Connor. I'm too heavy for this," I complain until I feel his mouth latch onto my clit as he growls against me. "Oh. My. God!"

He doesn't stop. His tongue glides from my entrance to my clit, lapping up my arousal. I'm on the verge of coming, my thighs trembling and clenching around his head when he abruptly stops. I groan in frustration when I feel a sudden vibration from his wicked laughter between my legs that sends me nearly over the edge. Before he allows my climax, he pulls back, pressing a soft kiss against my pubic bone, and slides a hand to my entrance. His thick fingers slowly slip inside me. I buck against his face as he fills me.

"Fuck, baby!" I moan.

My breathing is heavy as he slowly slides his fingers in and out of my slick channel. His tongue swirls around my clit in a deliriously slow motion, and I feel the moment his fingers hit that sweet spot he loves to tease until I lose all control. I realize I'm going to detonate mere seconds before it happens. I feel the gush between my legs, and his tongue goes into overdrive, flicking my clit like it's his damn job as my climax takes on a life of its own and continues well after it's usually over.

I finally come down, but he's still licking me, cleaning up the mess he caused.

We make it to Liam and Kayleigh's with only five minutes to spare before anyone else gets there. As soon as Daisey sees Connor, she leaps into his arms.

"Uncle Connor!" she squeals.

"Hey, sweet girl. I told you I'd be the first to get here. I'd never break a promise to you." He smiles at her and winks at me.

My ovaries suddenly wake up, going into overdrive at the sight before me.

Brady walks around the corner, and his eyes light up when he sees me. "Aunt Hadley! You're here! I have to show you what Aunt Jana and I made!"

He takes my hand, pulling me to his room where a Lego Stark Tower that is nearly my height stands front and center.

"Holy shit," I gasp when I see it.

"To the jar, Aunt Hadley!" he giggles.

Some time later, we sit around the kitchen table of Kayleigh and Liam's home that they share with Lance and Joel, giving toasts of well wishes and celebrating their anniversary. Kat and Ryan sit across from me. Jackson is next to Ryan, his arm draped around the back of her chair, as he casually plays with her hair. I raise a questioning brow at Kat, who just shrugs.

Kayleigh reiterates my favorite story of their relationship, which stars my favorite little man, Brady, and the reason why Connor will forever be known as my moose.

I glance over at Liam and Kayleigh, their intense love filling the room. A realization comes over me when I look back at Connor standing next to me.

"You know, you may have been my unexpected match, but no matter what I've gone through to get myself to this point, I would do it a hundred times over if it led me to you." I wrap my arms around his neck and stretch onto my toes to press my lips against his.

"Mo stór," he replies, his hands cupping my cheeks as he presses his forehead to mine. "Tá tú foirfe."

The End

While Hadley & Connor's story may be over, you'll see them again in Ryan & Greyson's story, *The Unexpected First*.

Interested in Kayleigh and Liam's story? Check out the novella *Endgame*, out now.

Acknowledgements

To Cristina, who encouraged me to follow a dream long forgotten. You have been there since the first words were written and stuck with me all the way through. I adore you and appreciate your friendship so much!

My alpha readers, Alanys & Danielle. Hadley and Connor's story has grown into so much more because of the love that you have shown them and me while I created their story. Let's shout it out one last time: "Fuck Andy!"

Sara - My boo. I'll forever be thankful that you slid into my DM's. You are phenomenal, and I love you!

To the FBI Agent who tracks my search history, it's been real.

Lastly, but most definitely not least, to every single one of you who has reached this page. There will never be enough words for me to express my love for you adequately. Thank you for reading this book. I cannot wait to share additional stories with you!

Also by

Firework - Prequel MM (Joel and Lance's story) coming soon

Endgame

The Unexpected Series

The Unexpected Match Hadley & Connor's Story

The Unexpected FirstRyan and Greyson's Story

The Unexpected Reunion - MFF - Coming soon

The Unexpected Second Chance- Coming soon

Stand Alone - Dark Romance

KILLER IN OUR POCKET - MFF

Stand Alone – Small Town Romance

Pumpkin Spice and Mr. Right

About the Author

I'm an introvert. Well, until you get to know me. Then I won't shut up. I'm married to my favorite PITA; he's the doctor to my Clara.

(IYKYK). We have a little boy who is growing way too fast and is already way too smart for my own sanity. I've had an unhealthy obsession with *Gilmore Girls* and *Buffy the Vampire Slayer* for years. You'll see the references throughout my writing. I've loved reading for as long as I can remember, but physical books with traditional novel paper give me the ick! So, you'll find me reading on my Kindle or listening to audiobooks on the regular.

Be sure to stalk me on all of my socials here